A KILLER WITHIN

THE SPIRIT WALKER SERIES

BOOK 2

DUANE WURST

ISBN-978-0-9883947-7-3

Text and cover design by Duane Wurst, Berne Studio
Cover images © Duane Wurst

Printed in the United States of America

ACKNOWLEDGMENTS

This story began when I was a child. I kept dreaming that someday, someone would dig up the skeletons I buried in my backyard. Perhaps they were just dreams, or perhaps they were real. I have been known to have my dreams come true and that scares me.

To death...

My ghosts... My deeds...

Floating in the universe for all time...
the spirits of Mankind are everywhere.
The flower, spider, badger, ant.
All a part of us,
because we are a part of Gods Creation.
And God, according to some, created it all.
One God... One Earth...
God, here I am...
talking to ghosts.

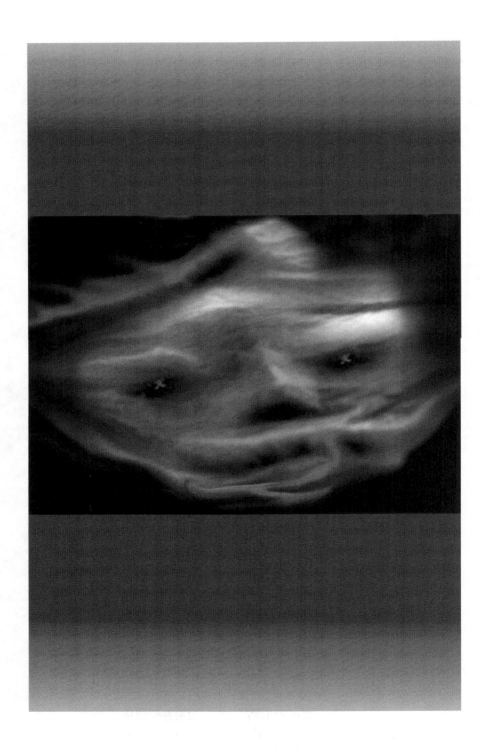

CHAPTER 1

Dr. Jahosibad told Harry to sit in the brown leather chair. "It is very comfortable." He took his notebook, wrote something, and said, "Harry, start from the beginning and tell me what you want to confess to the police."

Harry took a deep breath and began. "I was ten years old when the killings started. Our family lived in a small country house, a mile south of Bad Axe. Dad bought the house from a farmer who said the house came with the land he purchased a few years before. The farmer knew the little house would be a good starter home, and he needed the extra cash from its sale. The previous owners were unknown.

"Dad and Mom worked for another farmer, a mile down the road, and dad couldn't afford much. The house wasn't fancy. A cold and wet basement with two floors above, and four small bedrooms. I got to sleep upstairs, where there was no heat or running water. Mom and Dad slept downstairs. There was a small bathroom next to their room.

"Like I said, it was old and dirty, but Mom loved the house. She told dad she would clean, decorate, and make it into a good home. Dad bought the house with all of his meager savings, and he would have to pay the farmer twenty dollars a month for five years to pay the balance.

"Back then, I couldn't care less where I slept, as long as the bed was soft with blankets. At ten years old, I was kind of shy and spent a lot of time alone with Mom."

The doctor reached for Harry's arm and said, "Sir. We only

have an hour and you're walking us away from the problem, again. Now tell me more about the dreams you have been having."

He jotted another note on his tablet as Harry continued. "It began with a vivid dream I had one night. In the dream, I was burying a dead body behind our house. When I woke, I remembered the dream, but then I forgot. Later I had the dream again, and when I woke up, I was standing at the window looking down at the backyard. I soon knew this was more than just a stupid dream.

"I went back to being the obnoxious kid, figuring it was just a part of growing up. Everyone has crazy dreams. Hell... I was as normal as all my friends!

"The dreams didn't stop... and now they were being mixed with some dandy sexual ones. But the ones I remembered were the ones that repeated. I figure those dreams must mean more; otherwise, why would you dream them?"

The doctor nodded to continue. "Go on, but keep on topic."

Harry smiled and gazed toward the window. He could see nighttime approaching. "It got so bad that I hated sleeping at home and would ask to go with my friends, and I coaxed Mom into letting me stay overnight. I would have killed to end those dreams and to never see another dead body.

"I told my best friend Judy about my dream problems, and she laughed and said I was nuts.

"'Honey,' Judy moaned while rubbing my leg with her hand. 'You could kill no one. You just try to act macho, but you're a big teddy bear, deep down.'"

Harry raised his voice and turned to the doctor. "I never told another person, until today. It's been my dirty little secret, but now I have to confess. I know I buried sixteen bodies in the back yard, and I'm convinced I killed each of them."

Dr. Jahosibad smiled, and with kindness in his voice, he said, "And I appreciate the courage it's taken for you to open up like this. I am sure I can help you, Harry. In fact, your condition should respond to treatment, like the session we are having today, and I have several medications that can ease cases like this."

The doctor checked his notes and jotted something down. He smiled and said, "Please continue. I sent a message to my staff that I will be late tonight. We are making excellent progress, and if we spend another hour-long session, we may have a breakthrough tonight. So, please continue your tale."

Harry took a deep breath. He was getting tired and wished the session would end soon. He smiled at Dr. Jahosibad and continued, "The dreams didn't come around as often as I grew older, but when I was in high school I had terrible visions of Dad or someone else digging a hole where I buried a body. In fact, I convinced Dad to put a new septic tank to the side of the house instead of the backyard and directed contractors to avoid some of the burial plots.

"I had to think hard when Mom insisted I bury her dead cat where a young girl lay underground. I tried to remember where I buried the little box I put her in, and I aimed my shovel with great care. The shovel slid down the side of the girl's burial box; I could feel it scraping against my shovel, but Mom didn't notice.

"Mom, are you sure I have to bury it here?' I begged. Mom never saw a thing, but I was sweaty and cold and wanted to die. How could I be killing these people? I was just a stupid teenager, not good looking, not smart, and not lucky with girls.

"By the time high school came around, I had buried and probably killed ten people. I knew I had to get away, so I studied hard, earned great grades, and got a full ride to the University of Michigan. As soon as I moved away to attend college, the dreams and killings stopped. Actually, the dreams changed. Fear took over my mind. Fear that someone would dig behind my parents' old house and find the bodies I buried there as a kid. I became obsessed that I would be exposed for what I did, and I would have to go to prison.

"It was difficult having those memories and fears. As time passed, I thought less about the bodies and graves behind that little house in Bad Axe. Even if they dug up the yard, it wouldn't matter. Dad and Mom were never there. They moved to Port Austin and just kept the house for a hunting cabin. See, there's a nice stand of woods out behind, and Dad made enough working in the factories and in the stock market to buy that land for hunting.

"I worried less and studied hard. After getting my law degree, I became a professional cover-up artist... able to hide my fear, doubt, and pain. I pushed the fears behind me. There will always be the fear; however, my mind became set on having a future."

"When did you marry?" asked the Doc.

"About three months after I got my own office at the law firm, I met Kathy. I had a minor accident and met her in the ER. She was a doctor in training; she became a family doctor. We got married on a Friday and our honeymoon lasted till the following Monday, when we both headed back to work. We were so busy we didn't even take the time to have a family.

"I think she blamed me for that problem. I was good in bed and wanted sex all the time, but she said I never produced quality sperm. She gave me some medication to try, but I knew I was... you know... shooting blanks."

Dr. Jahosibad laughed. "I love your quaint play on words. So while you were in your childless marriage, were you faithful? Be honest. I can't help you if you don't tell me everything."

Darkness filled the window, but Harry couldn't tell how late it was, so he checked his cell phone for the time. The doctor reminded him not to use the phone, and Harry slipped it back into his pocket. He took a long sip of water and cleared his throat.

"Don't worry. I heard the question. I'm just thinking about my words... guess it's both what I should tell you and what I don't want to tell you that's causing me to rethink this whole situation. Psychiatrists all try to tie our problems with how our moms and dads raised us.

"Well... no one abused me as a child... no, I never fantasize about killing while having sex, and no, I don't want to sleep with my dead mother. It's crazy talk, but that's how I've felt all my life. I got married to stabilize my life. I can only blame myself for what happened in my youth, and of course it affected my married life. My wife thought I had a split personality, the way I was with her sometimes. She said I was like a cheap shower, either hot or cold. You know, that's my biggest fear. Could I be awake now, but a killer in another life? Is that what happened when I woke up looking out the window... fully dressed with dirt on my shoes. Doc, do you know what I'm asking?"

The doctor reached out and touched Harry's hand. "Sir, we will answer that question soon enough. You do not show the classic signs of split personality. In fact, I hypnotized you on our first meeting and I did not detect another personality. That is not saying he or she isn't there... hiding from us all."

Harry looked puzzled at the doctor's statement. "When did that happen?"

"Last week, when we first talked. I often use hypnosis to find out if there are any underlying conditions I need to know of. You are not the person you present to the world, and I believe the repetitive dreams are more than dreams. They are actual memories. Now we need to discover if they are true or false memories."

"You mean... you think I killed all those people! Don't you?

Come on, you can tell me what you think. I know. It's true. I had to have killed them, but why don't I remember killing them? I just remember burying them. It's like I wake up, find the body, and bury it. But then I wake up and ask myself if it all was just a dream."

"Harry, there is always a reason for what happens, and if we dig deeper, we'll find it. I don't think you wanted to sleep with your mom. No, that's not the problem you have."

The doctor watched for Harry's response. There was none.

CHAPTER 2

*N*o, Harry thought. *I never wanted to sleep with my dad either. But I sure wish he would have treated me better than he did.*

He could see that the doctor was waiting for his comment. "I loved my dad, but he didn't like me. I think he feared or resented me because I was an only child, and my Mom's fragile little boy. You know, she treated me like a stupid little doll. Mom dressed me, groomed me, and taught me how to be manly... and yes, I know what you're thinking... and no, I'm not queer or whatever you call it these days.

"Besides... I never had time for those kinds of thoughts. I worked while I was in high school, and the only spare time I had... well... I must have been busy killing people so I could bury them in the backyard."

Harry put his hand to his face and rubbed his temples. "Doctor, we seem to be right back to where we started and I have to pee."

Harry pulled himself out of the leather chair, turned toward the restroom, and asked, "Dr. Jahosibad, why do you want me to stay for two full sessions? You told me it would take months of private sessions before I would see any improvement. Now you want me to stay late? All I'm doing is blabbering about myself. Perhaps you're the crazy one, here."

"Perhaps... yes... perhaps."

When Harry returned, he glanced at his watch and sped up his story; he didn't wait for the doctor to ask him, he just started to ramble on again.

He felt like his words were clearer. *Perhaps this talking crap is working,* he thought. *If I can get through this without going to jail, I will be OK.*

"My wife died last year... it was sudden... she had a massive heart attack. I know, it's crazy, being she was a doctor and all. But being a doctor doesn't make you healthy. Like they say, doctors always take care of everyone but themselves.

"Anyway, after my wife died, I decided I didn't want to live in the city. I loved the theatre and all the nice places to eat, but I didn't have any close family. All my friends in Ann Arbor were my wife's friends. They died with her.

"You know, I loved my wife very much because she kept me sane. I never had a bad dream during my married life. I became grounded and my life was meaningful. After I retired, we slowed down. But she wouldn't give up her private practice. She was always seeing one more patient. 'Honey, just one more, then I'll rest.' Then she died.

"My parents died many years ago, and now I have their huge cottage in Port Austin and the old homestead. For years, the only time I saw the old place was during hunting trips. Mom kept it looking just like it did when I was a teenager. Same grubby wallpaper, and only one little downstairs bathroom. I had to run downstairs every time I needed to pee.

"While on one of our hunting trips, I had flashes of the old memories and powerful feelings of panic, but only when I spent a few days sleeping in my old bedroom. It was never as bad as when I was a kid. I mean, no dead bodies lying around or anything like that.

"Last spring, I sold the house in Ann Arbor and moved into the house on Lake Huron, then last month I had to move out because of remodeling. The builders said it would take three months, so I moved into the old place... lots of room, nice woods, and a field of dead bodies in the backyard. That should make my summer very interesting... right?"

The doctor smiled. "Yes, interesting. This entire situation is interesting. I know it is a heavy burden and you want quick solutions, and I am sure we will find the answers you are seeking, but trust me... I want only what is best for you, and that is not confessing to the police. You see Harry, we don't know if the bodies are real, or just another element of your dreams."

CHAPTER 3

Dr. Jahosibad asked Harry to talk about the dreams he is currently having.

"Like I said, I moved into the old homestead and now I'm sleeping there every night, and every night I'm burying the bodies again, and worse yet, I dreamed of killing them, or at least learning how they died. One time, a few weeks ago, I awoke while standing outside... wondering how I got there.

"Doctor, I'll go insane if you can't stop this. If you can't stop me... or perhaps, I am already insane?"

Tears rushed into Harry's eyes and he wept. "I know what I've done. I see it every night and it has to stop. I am convinced... I have convinced myself that I need to confess and turn myself into the police. Doctor, I need you to help me find the courage to face my sins."

Dr. Jahosibad tried to comfort Harry. "We will end our session now." He picked up a bottle from his desk and continued, "I want you to take these pills; they will help you sleep without dreams, and if you've been sleepwalking, these pills will prevent that. Come back tomorrow afternoon and we will start over. I can use hypnosis again. I don't think you are a killer, and I don't think you have a split personality, and I know you are not a psychotic person. The more I know about what happened, the better I will understand how cure you."

Harry removed his hands from his face and looked at the doctor. "You're telling me what I am not. You need to tell me what I am."

"I know... I'm sorry... I don't know."

Harry stood and took his jacket from the stand. He slid the coat over his suit coat and shuffled toward the door. He looked back, and the doctor was entering notes on his tablet.

It was a long ride back to Bad Axe. Harry parked the car and walked around the house. Standing in the backyard, tears again fill his eyes. In his mind he sees every grave, every child, woman, teenage boy, and their grandfathers and grandmothers. It is as if he knew them forever. They are the part of his soul he wants removed. Like the cancer his wife, mother, and father died from.

In his heart he knows he couldn't have killed those people, but he did. There is no other explanation.

The pills worked and Harry spent the night experiencing no dreams. He was wide awake at seven and almost joyful. He ate breakfast and called Dr. Jahosibad to tell him the good news.

"Wonderful, Harry. Come in at three o'clock. Harry, take no more of those pills. They can be dangerous. A couple times a week is all you can take. I'm sorry, but I am sure we will have a breakthrough soon."

Harry was speeding to Dr. Jahosibad's office. It was only a thirty-minute drive, but he took a nap after lunch and slept so well he overslept. He called the doctor, so there wasn't a rush, but he continued to speed.

There was a handicapped parking space in front of the office, so he took it and felt guilty that he had a permit.

Today it was a convenience, because the lot was full of cars. *Must be a lot of crazy people in town*, he thought.

When Harry walked through the doors, he shuffled himself into the leather chair. The doctor was waiting in the office and said, "There is so much I want to get done this afternoon, and your being late is putting us behind."

"I'm sorry, Sir, but it was your fault. You gave me those pills, and when I took my nap, I didn't dream. No... I just overslept. It was wonderful." Harry smiled and chuckled, almost a belly laugh.

The doctor also laughed. When Harry relaxed, the doctor talked in a low voice... very comforting. Harry didn't realize it, but the doctor was hypnotizing him. In a few minutes he was staring blankly into space while the doctor set up his video camera and wrote notes on his tablet, but no smile... just thoughts, *I must learn why Harry is having these dreams.* A pained look consumed his face... it was the look of doubt.

Enthralled with Harry's problem, the doctor imagined the story could become a murder novel, only he was the main character. He thought, *The detective... no... copper... no... well, perhaps just the dedicated healer... The Doctor!* He smiled.

"Harry, listen to my voice. Fell yourself becoming relaxed, comfortable, and calm. Remember when you were ten years old?"

"Yes."

"I want you to go up to your room. Look out the window and then go to bed. Don't worry about the dreams, just tell me what you see, understand?"

"Yes, I gotta, pee. Let me run downstairs. Mom is snoring and daddy is laying on the couch, and the TV has that signal on it. You know, *no more TV tonight* signals. I think they call it a test pattern or something like that. My friend Ralph says you can get channels that stay on all night, but you gotta get your antenna up real high. High... That's funny. It makes me think of my peter getting higher. I know if I have to pee, 'cause it gets hard. It's always hard... I wonder why?"

"Harry, stop talking about your penis."

"Ha! Penis... You said a bad word. Mom don't like when I say things like that. She says I have to have a clean mouth for God. I wonder why God needs a clean mouth. Don't he have one of his own? Well, why doesn't he just use toothpaste?"

"Harry, go back to sleep and enter your dream world. Tell me what you're seeing."

The doctor watched Harry on the TV monitor. Every motion was being recorded. "You are asleep... restful... alone...."

The young Harry spoke, "Everything is misty, you know, like fog. I can see the woods, and there's a crippled old man there. He motions that I should come to him. I don't know. Mom says I shouldn't talk to strangers. But he looks friendly, I think he's a neighbor or something. He's got a beard and looks like a hard worker. Kind of like my dad. He must be a friend of my dad. I wonder if he knows Dad? 'Hey, Mister. You know my dad?'

"He's whispering to me. I have to help him. What the...? There's a box on the ground. I ask what's in it. 'Can I see inside the box?'

"He lifts the lid, and I see a little girl. Oh shit... she don't have an arm and her face is half gone. God, she's dead. What the hell? Why is he showing me this dead girl? I don't wanna be here. I try to run but he grabs my arm and yells, 'You can't run away from this, boy. This is your doing and you gotta take care of it. You understand, boy? Bury her. It's your fault she's dead, so you gotta take care of her. It's your job, boy!'"

"Calm down, Harry." The doctor put his hand on Harry's shoulder. "Young man, tell me what you are doing. You are relaxed..."

"It's still foggy and I can hardly see, but I take the shovel and I dig about a foot deep. 'That's not good enough, boy. Dig it deeper. You don't want to smell her rotting body, do you? If you don't bury her deeper, dogs will find her and she'll be on your porch stinking up the place. Then your parents will know what you did.'"

"Harry, you are back in your bedroom, asleep. It's several months later."

Harry continued, "I started dreaming of that little girl, every night... every night. It wouldn't stop. Sometimes, when I didn't dream it, I would daydream about what it means. My thoughts were consumed by that event, even the cartoons on TV couldn't stop me from thinking about it."

"Harry, skip through your memories and stop at another burial. You are asleep, deeply asleep." The doctor checked his monitor.

"Eighteen months later, I had to bury an old woman. The old man wasn't there again, so I looked in the box and she was really ugly and old. I mean real old. It was hard to tell how I killed her, but she was dead. I was in the backyard with the box in front of me, and I knew what I had to do. It took all night to dig the hole, but at least the creepy old guy didn't show up.

"It didn't make sense, and I would spend hours trying to figure out how I killed people 'cause I didn't remember anything. You know, I never dreamed about killing. I mean, how did I do this?"

The doctor stopped the camera. "Harry, you are awake now. Why don't you use the restroom and then we can continue? Do you want something to drink?"

As Harry got out of the leather chair, he said, "I could use a rum and coke, but coffee with cream will do. Did I say anything interesting? I kind of remember some of our conversation. I was just a kid, wasn't I?"

"Yes, we covered your first dreams and the second murder."

Harry walked down the hall. The doctor noted how slowly he walked and thought about his own father, who he seldom visited. He wrote a note on his tablet. *Call Mom and Dad.*

The doctor passed Harry in the hallway. "I'll be out in a few minutes. Your coffee is on the desk."

Harry picked up his coffee and noticed the doctor's tablet on the oak side table. He didn't want to, but he had to look at what was written on it. When he saw the last note, he smiled. His face quickly turned grim when he recalled the doctor's words: "The second murder."

CHAPTER 4

Harry sat in the leather chair before the doctor returned from the bathroom. The doctor sat down and wrote more notes. Harry stretched his long legs and asked, "Please tell me your first name? I feel strange just calling you 'Doctor.'"

"Of course. My name is Roger Jahosibad. My dad loved his new country, America; he admired Roy Rogers."

"In that case, shouldn't your name be Roy?"

"There was a language problem, so I got stuck with Roger." The doctor laughed and jotted a note on his tablet. Harry was already under the doctor's hypnotic spell, "You are thirteen years old, Harry; tell me about yourself and your dreams."

Harry stiffened his back. His face turned defiant, and he said, "Why do you need to know that crap, Roger. I know your type. All up in my face for this or that. Why can't you old farts leave me and my friends alone? We don't hurt anyone. I mean, shit, we just want to have a little fun."

The doctor remained calm and didn't respond to the harsh attitude Harry was projecting. "Harry, don't bring me into this. You're a thirteen-year-old teenager; just tell me what things you do."

"Me? I like to dress in blue jeans. My mom and dad make me wear dress pants and white shirts. I have two pair of jeans at my friend Tommy's place, so when we go chasing the chicks, I can change into them. Doc, do you like girls, or are you queer? I like girls, smoking, and beer... not in that order, though.

"You know what I don't like? I don't enjoy going home. I hate that place. It always smells like death, and I'm sure you know all about my little problem. Well, the only way I can survive is to get out. So here I am. I spend almost all my spare time away from home. My mom gets pissed at me... but hey, she can't control me anymore. I'm older now. I'm thirteen so I can take care of myself... don't need no mommy to push me around and Dad doesn't care what I do, as long as I stay out of his way.

"Anyway, I was telling you about the crap I go through when I'm home and fall asleep. Well... I'm killing another poor bastard and planting him in the backyard... It's killing me, Doc. Get the joke there? Kind of funny, isn't it? You're not laughing, are you?

"OK, be that way. I don't really want to hear from you, anyway. My opinions are the only ones that count. Mine and my friend Tommy's. Did I tell you we're buddies? We fish together, ride our bikes all around, but we don't really drink beer, often. I was just putting you on. The last time we drank was when we found six bottles of beer in the garage... they were old and stale. Tasted like piss, but we got drunk, nevertheless. The killing is real... it's so bad... I'm so bad. I hate myself and I want to die, Doc. Just pulling your leg. Had you going there, didn't I? Well?"

Putting his hands on Harry's shoulders, the doctor said, in a strong yet soothing voice, "It's OK, Harry. Move on. Tell me about the backyard?"

"You can't look there. If you find one of them, my secret will be out."

"I won't tell anyone, but you can tell me everything."

"The reason I stay away from home is that I dream and then I kill people. Well, I'm not sure I kill them, but I know I bury them... in the backyard. Tell me, is that crazy or what?

"One-day Tommy, my friend, was with me in the backyard, and I told him about the graves. He thought I was joking and so I let it go. No reason to lose my friendship just because I needed someone to confide in. When we got away from my house, he said he was creeped out by my backyard. I asked why, almost knowing the answer, and he said, 'It stinks like something died there. You know, like a dead rat in a rat trap. You can smell it, but you don't remember where you put the trap, so you follow the smell until it gets stronger... right in your nose, and you finally find it.'

"Doc. I don't want to talk about this. I hate the lies I live. I have to hide my feelings from everyone... my parents, friends, and teachers. I can't let anyone know who I am, what I am. Will I always have to live like this? When I become an adult, will it end? Will the dreams and lies ever end? Will the killings ever stop?"

The doctor wiped his eyes as Harry sighed and asked, "Why am I having these dreams? Is a part of me killing these people without me knowing? I saw a TV program about people like that. I think they said they were splits of something. Am I one of those people? If I am, could I plead insanity? I don't want to go to jail or some place for crazy people, Doc. I just want these dreams to stop so I can be normal. Can you help me do that... please?"

"Harry, you are awake now." The doctor paused and rubbed tears from his eyes. His face filled with thought, then a forced smile. "I better understand your turmoil, and I will change your life by stopping the dreams." He was being kind with his words.

CHAPTER 5

Harry walked to his car, sat for a few minutes... thinking. He reached for a water bottle behind his seat, twisted the cap off, drank, and after setting his radio to a hard rock station, he was on his way back to Bad Axe. The only way to keep the demons out of his mind now was music... loud enough to drown out the inner noise.

Instead of stopping at the family home, he drove to Port Austin to check the work being done on his home on the lakeshore... and then stopped for dinner and a drink at The Bank. Harry didn't want to go home. There was nothing for him there but the dead and buried... the dreams. He watched the other couples... as his mind drifted back to his wife, Kathy, and the love they shared before her death.

Harry mused, took a few deep breaths and sighed. *Kathy saved my life so many times... I remember being like the happy couples here. She took so much pain away from my heart... she made me smile.*

The cell phone buzzed. It was Harry's builder texting that the house on the lake won't be ready for another month.

He asked himself, *Can I make it?*

Harry's mind was awash with a softer, gentler daydream, as if sent to him by his wife. He and Kathy were together on the beach watching the sunset as a refreshing breeze swept across Lake Huron and cooled their overheated bodies. Just as Harry prepared to kiss Kathy, her cell phone rang. Kathy begged him to let her go back to Ann Arbor... to cut into a man. He wanted her to fix him.

"Honey, he needs me. He could die without this surgery," she pleaded, ready to burst into tears.

Harry turned her image off and stood over the grave site of the old man from Caseville. He was in his sixties, strong as hell, could whoop any man. Problem is, he's dead. His head cut off and laying beside him. Not too pretty, but Harry knew what he had to do. *BURY HIM.*

The waitress repeated her question as Harry looked up.

"No... nothing else." *Just a brain transplant*, he thought.

It was after ten when he returned to his home in Bad Axe. He walked around the house and ambled over to Caseville Man's grave. Standing on the grave, he closed his eyes and whispered, *I'm sorry.*

***

The drive back to the doctor the next morning, seemed shorter than the past days. *Perhaps it was last night's dream*, he thought. *Perhaps the doctor is helping. Perhaps he can cure me. Perhaps I am fantasizing.*

He checked his watch and decided he had enough time for a McDonald's breakfast. He went inside because he hated to drive and eat. The young girl at the register smiled, and he asked for his favorite Egg McMuffin meal, with coffee and cream.

Harry played with his phone while he waited for someone to bring his meal. As he scrolled through his Facebook messages, he noticed several new images. A young girl dressed in vintage clothing; an old man in a black coat, pants, and stovepipe hat; a woman of substantial proportions in front of an antique, wood-burning kitchen stove.

He stopped and stared at the images. He realized these were the people he buried when he was a teenager. Not as they looked when they were dead, but before he killed them.

Tears filled his eyes as a young girl brought his breakfast. "Is everything OK, Sir?" she asked.

"Oh, I'm fine. Must be allergies," he responded as he wiped his face with a white handkerchief. "Thank you for bringing my meal."

***

Dr. Jahosibad was standing at the door as Harry walked up the long sidewalk. "I saw you drive in," the doctor said. "Did you have a good night?" Without waiting for the answer, he said, "We have much to do today, so let's get started."

Harry pulled himself into the leather chair and sighed. "I had several dreams and memory flashes this morning. It seems like I am getting worse. Do you think I should move out of the old homestead?"

"That's your decision. I know the memory flashes started again because of your return home. You told me there were fewer instances of them during your adult life. Is that true?"

"Yes, while I was in college and during my life with Kathy, I seldom dreamt about the killings and burials. I did, however, feel tremendous guilt and fear. Every day I considered what will happen when someone digs up the backyard and finds the bodies I buried there."

"How did you deal with this fear?" The doctor jotted a note on his tablet as Harry considered his answer.

"I forced the thoughts out of my mind. During that time of my life, I had great control of my feelings, especially when I was with my wife. All I had to do to waylay my fears was to look at her. Her love filled my heart and together we pushed our pasts aside."

The doctor said, "Harry, go back to after you and Kathy married; tell me about your life together."

Harry stared at the doctor, smiled, and said, "We are always busy. Last week the head of the law firm, asked if I would consider a junior partnership position. Man, how could I refuse. I told Kathy about the promotion and she suggested we go out to dinner and celebrate. We always go out for dinner. I went on to become the head of the firm. I work about ten hours a day, and Kathy is still working in the emergency room at University Hospital in Ann Arbor... long hours and mind-numbing.

"We see each other between midnight and dawn. It's no wonder we can't have kids, there's no time. Kathy says she wants to have children, but she wants to wait until she has her own family medical practice."

Dr. Jahosibad interrupted, "Harry, do you want children? Please be honest with me."

"No! I can't subject a child of mine to the hell I've been living. I remember my childhood and the trauma I went through, and I'm still living with the results of my actions. When I think of passing my genes on to another being, I cringe in fear. What if the child is like me? What if he or she is another killer? How could I deal with that pain and guilt?"

Dr. Jahosibad allowed Harry to relax. There were many questions he wanted to ask, but....

The doctor was standing at his desk as Harry returned from the restroom.

"Harry, don't you hope you didn't kill those people?"

Harry walked up to the coat-rack and stopped. He turned his head back to the Doctor. "I don't know what I hope for anymore. Sometimes the hope is not there, just the pain."

***

Harry drove back to Bad Axe and contemplated the conversations he had with the doctor about why he doesn't have a split personality. *I mean, Sweet Jesus, I know there's at least two here,* Harry thought. Instead of driving to the homestead, he drove into town. It was late afternoon, but he figured the sheriff's office would be open, and Sheriff McNabb should be there.

Do I want to do this? he asked himself. *No, but I have to. Doctor Roger isn't getting the job done. Neither is my contractor in Port Austin.*

The lovely young blond said, "Cousin Harry, what are you doing here? Did you hit a deer? They're terrible this year."

"No Marge, I just need to tell the sheriff something. My psychiatrist doesn't want me to tell my story, but I can't take it anymore. Is McNabb in?"

"I'll walk down to his office. Wait here, I think he might be in a meeting, but we'll see."

The husky sheriff returned with Marge and took Harry's hand. "Harry, I understand you're distraught about something. Don't you think you should take Dr. Jahosibad's advice? You need treatments." McNabb turned to Marge. "I'll call the doctor... you see that Harry gets home. He needs to rest."

CHAPTER 6

The sunlight streamed into Harry's bedroom, like rays of hope for a better future. He was sleeping in his parents' old bedroom and felt refreshed. There were no memorable dreams. Harry's memories of yesterday's session and the drive home had become shaded. *I thought I was planning to see the sheriff, but... no... what did I do?*

A man's scream from the backyard broke the stillness of morning. Harry jumped up; he felt confused, pushed the back door open, and leaped off the porch in a single bound... colliding with his doctor.

Picking himself off the lawn, Harry barked, "You talked to the sheriff. I remember now. What the hell are you doing here? And why have you been talking to the sheriff?"

"Harry, I had to protect you. I knew you were ready to confess, and I had to stop you. I talked to Sheriff McNabb and told him you have a mental disease caused by old age that is killing you, and I wanted him to understand."

Harry turned away. "Are you serious? You know my mind is sharp; I don't have any illness... or is there something I don't see? And why did you scream?"

"No, you are fine. Harry, you are not crazy. I didn't scream. Why? Did you hear something?" Roger looked around the yard.

"Come in." With reluctance, Harry invited Roger into the house and offered a seat at the table. Harry looked out the window into the graveyard. *Must have been the Caseville Man,* he thought.

The doctor continued. "Harry, I know it's hard to believe, but I am positive there is something more going on here than dreams."

"You realize you're playing with my emotions, and I'm not sure why that doesn't make me feel more uncomfortable." The doctor's appearance puzzled Harry; he was unsure about having him in his house of horrors. In the past ten years, since his parents' deaths, Harry avoided inviting guests into the home. He set up camping sites for his friends and told them the old house was out of commission. Anything to avoid having a guest snooping around.

Eying Harry's single-serve coffee maker, the doctor said, "Harry, get me a cup of coffee with cream, and put it in a small mug. I like my coffee strong."

"Yes... of course you do... coffee. What are your plans? Perhaps you're writing a book about the crazy old man, or are you making an Amazon movie? Oh, hell... why not a TV series?"

"No. It is my intention to prove you are innocent." Roger reached out and took the mug from Harry's hand, smiled, and continued. "Let's talk. Everything revolves around your dreams. My job is to learn what they mean and how I can free you from their chains."

Harry laughed. At first it was a chuckle, then a belly laugh. "You idiot. Isn't that what I told you the first day we met?"

"Well... yes, but now I know you were right. Progress is progress."

Harry slouched into his chair and put his face on the kitchen table.

"I want to go to McDonalds for breakfast, or does Sheriff McNabb have to approve that too?"

Dr. Jahosibad knew he made a foolish mistake by not handling the sheriff in a better manner. "I'm sorry."

Harry made a stern face and growled. With a dusty voice he said, "Why aren't you afraid of me? You know I might be a killer, and I buried sixteen people back there." Harry pointed out the back window.

The doctor smiled. "Yes, and I want you to mark all the graves. All sixteen. I have grave markers in the trunk of my car. I'll get them if you make me another mug of coffee."

The thought of marking the graves made Harry shudder. *I've been hiding them for all these years and now he wants me to put a sign on each grave? I might as well just have the sheriff come over to watch the circus.*

The doctor's coffee was on the table when he returned from his car. He had a burlap sack filled with white wooden crosses, each eighteen inches tall. He opened the large sack and handed one to Harry. "We can write who the dead person is on the cross."

"I don't know their names. Doctor, this is getting a little silly, isn't it?" Harry asked. *Why did I make that first appointment with Jahosibad? This will not go well,* he thought.

The doctor laughed. "Don't worry so much. A brief description is all I want... like *Caseville Man*, you told me about him, and the huge old lady... so we know where to dig."

"Dig?" Harry gasped. "We can't dig them up... not now. Jesus, what are you trying to do? Push me over the edge?"

"No. You can handle this." The doctor grabbed Harry's shoulders. "Trust me, it will be OK."

The doctor finished his coffee and instructed Harry to carry the sack of markers. "Come along, we need to get this done."

Harry complied and walked into the yard. It was a cool, overcast summer morning. "Do you want the graves marked in the order I buried them?"

"Yes, that would be good. You said the first was a young dismembered girl, right?"

"Yes..." A tear ran down Harry's cheek as he approached the girl's grave. He fell to his knees and pulled a cross from the sack. Dr. Jahosibad handed him a black marker.

Harry thought for a moment... then he wrote the number 1, a dash, and... *little broken girl.* He pushed the cross into the soil.

There was the soft sound of wind rushing from the ground up the cross, passing Harry's hand, arm, shoulder... it flashed across his face, reminding Harry of all the times he stood over a grave and shoveled dirt onto a crude casket.

The doctor put a hand on Harry's shoulder. "See, that wasn't so bad. Now, where is the second grave?"

Harry stood with some effort, pulled himself across the yard, and wrote on another cross... number 2 Baby 1. He pulled another cross out and wrote number 3 Baby 2. He pushed one into the soil and placed another cross next to it.

The doctor wrote the information on his notepad. With a puzzled look he said, "You told me the second burial was an old lady; why didn't you tell me you buried two babies?"

Harry softly mumbled, "I try to forget. It hurts too much to think that I might have killed two babies."

The doctor didn't respond.

The two men continued for an hour until all sixteen crosses had exposed the souls below.

Harry started back to the house, turned, and looked at the yard with the tiny markers dotting it. The Caseville Man, with his head under his arm, stood over his grave and yelled, "You can't do this to us, Harry."

Harry screamed, "NO! Stop! I can't betray their trust. I can't."

"Harry," the doctor whispered. "It's too late to stop. Let this happen. I know it hurts, but like a sliver, we must excise it from your being. That's how we heal."

The two returned to the kitchen. Harry looked back and saw

all sixteen victims standing over their graves. He could hear the muffled cries... "Don't... Help us... Stop... You can't betray…"

CHAPTER 7

The doctor helped Harry to the kitchen table. He pulled a chair out and guided the old man into it.

Harry regained his composure. "Thank you, Roger. Thank you for making me face these demons. I guess I am insane... a psychopathic killer, but it just doesn't fit." He ran his hand across the tabletop, sweeping a few letters and bills onto the floor.

The startled doctor came forward, bent down... put his mouth close to Harry's ear, and said, "Harry, what makes little sense?"

"I don't know. I just don't know, and that makes little sense."

"You don't know what?" The doctor stood back, waiting for the answer.

"I'm seeing ghostly images of the people I buried. They have been showing up, in and around the backyard, all month. Why do they expect me to help them? They keep begging for my help. They want me to stop. Stop what? Stop blaming myself for killing them?"

"You didn't kill them," the doctor insisted. "What did you see when you looked back into the yard?"

"They were standing on their graves. They looked like they did when I buried them, and everyone but the babies were there... yelling at me."

"What did they say?"

"Please don't... Please help us..." Harry stood and walked to the coffeemaker. "Do you want another coffee, Doctor?".

"Don't you want to know what your vision means? We need to talk about these hallucinations, now. We are getting closer and you want coffee?"

"No. I asked if you want coffee." Harry opened the refrigerator and took out a container of vegetable juice. He reached for a glass from the top cupboard and poured the juice. "I already know what it means. It means I'm a crazy old man and I need to be in jail where I can't harm anyone."

"Don't be ridiculous, Harry. You are as sane as I am."

"Then you're a crazy doctor," Harry said with a chuckle. "Look, I buried sixteen people in the backyard and now I'm seeing their ghosts. How is that sane?"

"I don't know, but you are sane, and I know the difference between sane and insane. Harry, trust me, I don't think there are any bodies in the backyard. I don't think you killed anyone. This all started when you were ten years old. You were a strong, tall youngster... starting puberty. You had a dream and fixated on it. In your young mind it became so real that you obsessed over whether those dreams were your reality. That is not normal and a good counselor could have helped you see that, if you had asked for help. But, no... you were secretive. You told no one about the dream, and like most obsessions, it took control of your life. And yes, I will have another coffee. After we finish here, we will dig in the yard, and you will see there are no dead bodies."

Harry shuddered at the idea, but he nodded approval. Sixty years of living in hell, protecting the secrets buried in the backyard, Harry thought. I guess it is time to uncover the poor souls and free them.

Dr. Jahosibad finished his coffee and stood. "Are you ready? Where is your shovel?" he asked.

Harry stood and opened a door leading to the basement. "There's one downstairs," he said.

The doctor listened to the steps creaking down and then

climbing back up. "You keep your shovel in the basement?"

"Yes, it makes me think twice about using it, besides this one has been here ever since I was a kid. It was Dad's shovel." He dusted off the handle and opened the back door. "Well?"

"Yes, I'm coming," said the doctor.

As the two men walked into the backyard, Harry stopped at the grave of the first victim. The young girl severed into pieces, her head crushed, and one arm missing. He could hear rustling. The wind? he asked himself. Then he saw the old woman from Bad Axe. She was overweight, elderly, and wore a dress like his mother used to wear. Full around the hips and hanging down to the ground. Her hands were covered in dirt... as if she dug her way out of the ground.

Harry looked at Dr. Jahosibad and asked, "You don't see her, do you?"

"See who? Tell me who and where she is," he insisted.

"She's the Bad Axe woman, Clara, Number 4. I remember how hard it was rolling her into the box. She must have weighed 250 pounds at least."

The doctor followed Harry's outstretched arm and finger and tried to see what he was seeing. Nothing. No mist, no old woman, just the silent yard, sun streaming through the trees making the white crosses glisten.

"I know you can't see her, but she's talking to us... Listen..."

"You must tell me, because I can't hear her, either." The doctor moved closer to Harry so he could hear him speak.

Harry began repeating her words. "Please don't hurt us, Harry. If you do this, we can never rest. We need you to protect us. We're your secrets. Do you want to expose us to the world? Keep us hidden... Don't do this... if you do you will pay, Son."

Dr. Jahosibad shook his head. "Does she remind you of your mother? Is that why she calls you son? Perhaps she is your mother?"

"No... she's gone now, and she wasn't anything like my mother," Harry said as he walked to the side of the house and grabbed a wicker chair. He pulled it to the little broken girl's grave site and sat down.

"You can't sit down; you must dig up the girl's grave," the doctor insisted.

"Like hell... your idea... your job. I'm sitting here and watching." The doctor took the shovel and pushed it into the ground next to the white cross. Harry heard a scream from the little girl. Such a painful scream that tears ran down his cheeks as he watched the shovel pull scoop after scoop of earth from the ground, accompanied by the wailing of a tragic young girl.

The doctor kept digging, finding nothing. "See, Harry, there is not a body here. Do you see now that you based your obsession on the dream?"

"Keep digging. I should have buried her six feet down, but I settled at three feet. You're only about two feet deep, now." Harry crossed his legs and stared at the doctor as he threw mounds of dirt over the edge of the deepening hole.

"I hit something, Harry." The doctor looked over the edge at Harry, now standing over the grave... watching the doctor. "Sounds like wood. Yes, it's wood." He continued digging and bent down. "Oh God, no. There are bones mixed with the wooden shards. I can't keep digging, Harry. I have to stop. We must preserve the evidence for the authorities. I'm sorry, Harry, perhaps you are a killer."

CHAPTER 8

Harry put his hand out and helped pull the doctor to the surface. "So this is it? Now we call Sheriff McNabb and tell him everything?"

"Let's talk in the house. I hate having dirt on my hands and I need to wash up. We can talk later."

Harry chuckled. "You don't know what to do, do you?" he chided. "I told you I buried the bodies here. Now you believe me... right?"

The doctor looked back at the yard and sighed. "I don't know what to believe, Harry. I don't think you are a killer, but I'm perplexed. Let's talk over a drink. I need something stronger than coffee; do you have beer, wine, or scotch?"

"Yes, all three."

Harry put two cold beers on the table while the doctor went down the hall to use the bathroom. Waiting, Harry took his beer and stood at the window, watching the backyard. The ghostly images of the dead gathered around Caseville Man as he talked. Harry couldn't hear their voices, but he could tell they were upset.

"Harry, what's on your mind? You appear to be miles away."

"The dead are holding a meeting at the far end of the yard. They act like they're making plans to revolt or something. You stirred up a hornet nest, doctor."

"Are you seeing them, now?" the doctor asked, as he looked over Harry's shoulder and watched the empty yard. "I see nothing there but some birds on the ground where I dug. Robins looking for worms in the tilled soil."

Harry sat at the large oak table and took a sip of his beer. "Have you decided what we should do next? You know I'm ready to turn myself in to the authorities whenever you let me. I would do it myself, but you seem to have the sheriff under your spell... so, what do you suggest?"

"We need to wait. Confessing to the sheriff is the last resort. I need more time with you, Harry. You're a lawyer... you know how slow the system works. I want to learn everything... your past, present, and future. It's important." The doctor looked down, considering his words. "You've had your entire life affected by whatever this is. I want to help you, but I also want to know the truth. My reasons are complicated, like your life."

Harry smiled. "What more do you need to know?"

"In our sessions, I noticed you have a few lost memories from your early childhood. These lapses of memory often result from an occurrence that we wanted to forget. Perhaps you have memories of childhood events that you have not shared? Most likely involving traumatic incidents like... perhaps a family death, a fight, or even an illness. Something blocked the memory and that event may have led to your obsessions."

The doctor finished his beer and added, "I'm not saying you didn't bury those people, but I still doubt that you could have buried sixteen bodies without your parents noticing. I mean, wouldn't they have asked about the fresh dirt? Look outside, see the mess I made of your lawn. Now times that by sixteen and picture your parents not seeing that."

"Odd... I never thought about that. You make a strong case for continued therapy, but now we should cover up the little girl in the backyard, so she can sleep tonight."

"No, I want to make a few calls to a woman I know in Ann Arbor. I want more information on the girl's remains. My friend is a forensic scientist and she studies bones for the university archaeology department. She can study the bones and tell us about the person and perhaps how they died. I want to make sure they match what you have told me about the child. My friend, Caroline Hyde, will do this without reporting to the sheriff. If I ask someone local, the sheriff will hear about it and start investigating before we have the answers."

"OK. Call her, if you must, but they won't like it." Harry turned to the window... the ghosts were gone. I wonder if they heard the doctor? he asked himself.

Doctor Jahosibad walked to his car and returned with his laptop. He made a temporary work area on the kitchen table, while Harry showered and changed into brown dress slacks and a cream and brown golf shirt.

When he returned, the doctor was just finishing a phone call. "Good news. Caroline can be here tomorrow morning. She is excited by the tale I told her. Is it OK if she stays for a few days? She's bringing the university mobile lab and can do her investigations right here."

"Isn't she afraid I might snap and add two more bodies to the graveyard?"

"Hilarious, Harry. No... we are not afraid." The doctor gathered his papers and put the computer back into its leather case. "I told her you would be fine with having guests."

"I take it you're staying here too?"

"Yes, I intend to spend a few days here, as is Caroline. We want to solve this mystery, before we leave your home."

"You seem confident. It's taken me fifty years to tell someone about my troubled past, and yet, you intend to find all the answers in a few days." Harry's voice had a cynical tone, as he intended. The pace of Doctor Jahosibad's investigations disturbed him, and he wished there was more time to deal with the ghosts. Over time, they became his family, and he has a strong sense of responsibility. Not just for their murders, but for their spiritual path to the beyond. If their God exists, why did he lead me into this mess? Shit, what the hell possessed me to become a teen killer?

The doctor put his hand on Harry's arm to bring his attention back to their conversation. "Harry, I am confident and hungry. Can you suggest a restaurant where we can get lunch?"

Harry and the doctor climbed into Harry's car and headed to Bad Axe. The two enjoyed a relaxing lunch at China King. The doctor wished he had a glass of wine with his meal, but he raved about the food.

As they ate, Harry thought about his childhood and tried to remember all the times he faced traumatic experiences. His mind returned to the crimes he committed... the deaths he took part in. The trauma the doctor talks about could be the trauma I would have faced when I killed them. *Perhaps that is the memory I am blocking. God... what if...?*

CHAPTER 9

Harry's car approached the white farmhouse. Dread and panic came over him, and he tightly gripped the wheel. The doctor noticed Harry's reaction and asked, "What is it?"

"They're standing in the driveway, blocking our path."

The doctor saw nothing. No birds, small animals, or ghosts. "Drive through them, Harry. They're NOT real."

Harry drove down the path... the ghostly figures moved to the side, allowing him passage. After he stepped out of the vehicle, he looked back and saw only the Caseville man, standing with his head tucked under his arm... his eyes staring at him... staring into his soul... eyes filled with pain and anger.

Tears overwhelmed Harry. He turned and followed the doctor as he strolled toward the house, occasionally looking back at Caseville Man.

"Harry, lunch was lovely, both the food, the atmosphere, and the company. I saw you were in deep thought throughout our meal. Do you have anything you want to share with me?"

"Yes, I suppose I do. I was thinking about the missing memories you say I have. Could they be the memories of my killing these people? Perhaps I have blocked those memories and left only the memories of the burials."

"That crossed my mind." The doctor's eyes strayed toward the tops of the trees. He watched as a woodpecker tapped at a dead branch and two squirrels chased another, who raced across the branches with a stolen walnut in his mouth. "I think you should know what my diagnosis is?"

Harry didn't respond, so the doctor continued, "Harry, you are an intellectual man, and I want to be up front. There isn't time for games, you know what I'm saying?"

"Yes, tell me. Be honest... brutal if need be."

"Your obsession began when you were a child. You suffer from dream-reality confusion (DRC). Your dreams were so real that you soon became unable to distinguish between reality and your dream state. This happens when you also are suffering from borderline personality disorder (BPD)."

Harry smiled. "Well, now we're getting down to the nitty-gritty of my reality. So I'm not normal, am I?" Harry chuckled. He recalled reading about the diagnosis the doctor suggested. Through the years, Harry spent thousands of hours self-diagnosing his problems. At least the doctor had reached a conclusion that he also found plausible.

"Do you think my visions of the dead are daydreams? Am I so fragile that I am moving between reality and the dream state... minute by minute?"

"Yes, I think what started as a sleep and dream disorder has become a personality disorder. You are not crazy, per se. Through the years, as a defensive mechanism, you protect yourself by hiding within and from your dreams, which have become intertwined with your reality. You see ghosts now, because you have lost your ability to control the dream/reality relationship. You are a man with memories, which you can no longer run away from, and that is tearing you apart."

Harry's face turned solemn as tears filled his eyes and ran down rugged cheeks, splashing onto the table with the crescendo of Tahquamenon Falls. With every tear came a sense of relief that he finally shared his burden with another being. Relief that, perhaps, he can die knowing the truth. A cleansing relief that he feared would be short lived.

After a restless night, Harry took a long hot shower, and then remembered he still had a guest in the house. He looked out the bathroom window... in the back corner of the yard, Caseville Man was talking with Farmer Bill. Harry could feel their eyes glancing toward the window. He senced they knew he was watching them, and a chill filled the room.

I haven't seen Farmer Bill in years, Harry thought. *Bill died a horrible death. Burned in a field of straw.* In Harry's mind there is a hazy memory of striking a match, but there is a vivid memory of digging the grave... *tall man, extra-long grave. The man smelled like cooked pork*, Harry recalled. A slight grin flashed over his lips. Not an evil grin... no, a "that's funny" grin.

"Harry, I need to use the toilet. Could you hurry?"

"Doc. Just go outside if you can't hold it."

Harry suddenly realized he was being crass and apologized as he collected his belongings. "Roger," he poked his head into the hallway, "you can use the bathroom; I'll get dressed in the bedroom."

Roger collected himself and quickly scooted toward the toilet, pushing the door shut as Harry left the room wearing only a small towel. The doctor shouted through the closed door, "By the way, Caroline Hyde, the forensic scientist I told you about, will be here in less than an hour. She called and left a message."

Harry heard the doctor, but didn't respond. His mind was on the residents of his graveyard. Over the years he's gotten to know each victim. They're too real to be just a dream.

Staring into the closet, Harry wondered what to wear. Blue jeans, again? Didn't the doctor say the woman would be here soon? I wonder if she's single, good looking, and into older guys?

He decided on a black polo shirt and black jeans. It made him feel slimmer and more confident with women. His wife always laughed at his somber clothing choices. "Can't you just try something bright?" she would ask.

Happy, that would be the day, he mused. Black it is, and black deck shoes it will be. She won't see me coming, especially in the dark.

While the doctor finished his shower, Harry checked his phone for messages and the news. Nothing exciting, he thought. I guess there's more action in the back yard, than the rest of the world. Imagine what it will be like when the great Doctor Roger Jahosibad reveals he has discovered a serial killer hiding in the small town of Bad Axe. That should hit the local and national news. Then... the entire world will know my little secret.

The thought made him shiver. The entire world, and God. Again he grinned. I imagine God already knows what I've done.

CHAPTER 10

Harry sat at the kitchen table, sipping hot coffee. The impending arrival of Caroline, the forensic scientist from Ann Arbor, filled his mind with doubt, apprehension, and a not-so-strange excitement encompassing his groin. He heard her name mentioned prior to the doctor's decision to bring her into the investigation and was told she was a looker and a genius.

Roger walked through the kitchen in his white underwear, showing his impressive bulge. Harry smiled, and he felt that stirring again. *Strange*, he thought, and laughed.

The doctor looked out the back window. "Are your ghosts still walking around?" he asked.

"Yes, I saw Farmer Bill. He was a burn victim and rarely shows up here or in my dreams. I'm not sure why, perhaps because I feel I knew him other than by burying him."

"So you remember killing him?"

"I'm not sure, but I remembered how he smelled when I dropped him into the hole."

"Smelled?"

"Like barbecued pork."

Roger let out a stifled laugh. "God Harry, that's sick. Funny, but sick."

"I know, and so is walking around in your underwear."

Roger looked down and with surprise replied, "Sorry, I forgot I wasn't home. I'll get dressed." He rushed out of the room, keeping his hands in front of him. Harry could hear the bedroom door shut as he let his mind wander into the past. His mom stood at the stove tending bacon, hash-browns, and eggs. The eggs were from the chicken coop he took care of, and the bacon came from his dad's boss, Farmer Joseph.

"Harry, I heard you up last night. Did you have stomach trouble again?"

"No, Mom. I just couldn't sleep because of another nightmare."

"That's not surprising... you ate a lot of cheese last night. They say cheese will cause nightmares. Avoid cheese and all your problems will disappear. Honey, you want a slice of cheese on your egg?"

"No." The irony was not lost. "When did Dad leave for work?"

"He didn't come home last night. I think he slept in the bunkhouse with the guys at the farm. He must have worked late," she said. Harry could tell she was hiding something. At only thirteen, he was mindful of her feelings.

"Did I tell you this morning how much I love you? I'm sure I did, but just in case, I do."

"Harry," the doctor interrupted. "What's for breakfast?"

"Bacon and eggs, but shouldn't we wait to see if our guests have eaten?"

The doctor picked up his phone and checked his messages. "Caroline is about five miles from here. So, yes, let's wait for them." He put his phone down and asked, "Do you have enough food for four more people?"

"Yes, I always keep the pantry well-stocked. It's an old habit." Harry put the bacon and eggs back in the refrigerator and refilled his coffee cup. "What three people are with her?"

"She brought her assistant, Jonathon, and Lila, and her grandson, Charlie... eighteen, a sophomore at Michigan, and lives with Caroline. Caroline's daughter, Diana, passed when Charlie was young. She refused to say who fathered him."

"I hope you don't expect me to cook and feed everyone... for how long, or did you say?"

"I didn't, and I don't know. It will all work out, Harry. Just remember, we're here to help you sort out this mystery. If you don't want our help, just speak up." The doctor hesitated and prayed Harry didn't listen to him at this moment. "I mean, for your sake, you must let us help you. You know that, don't you?"

"Yes, Roger. Remember, I was the one who contacted you. I started this quest for the truth. I am the one who needs to be set free."

"Good," the doctor said as he looked through the kitchen-door window and saw a huge motorhome pull into the yard, followed by a large windowless van and trailer. "They're here, Harry."

Harry had already walked to the door, having heard them approach before Roger saw them. He opened the door as he grabbed his jacket and walked into the yard. Caroline was instructing the driver of the van where he should park.

She turned to Harry and yelled, "You must be Harry, I'm Caroline. Is there anywhere we can't park?"

"Don't get too close to this side of the house; that's where the septic tank is located."

"And I hear the backyard is where you buried your bodies?"

Her bluntness surprised Harry. "Yes, my bodies are in the backyard." Hearing himself speak the words gave him a chill. He turned to look toward the graves and gasped... Farmer Bill stood next to him. *That's why I have chills*, he thought.

Farmer Bill was talking, but Harry didn't listen. He closed his ears and walked toward the vehicles and his new guests.

CHAPTER 11

Harry walked to the motorhome. Caroline was standing next to the door, watching as he approached. In a tender voice, she said, "It's beautiful, isn't it?"

Harry wasn't sure what she meant. Then he noticed her admiring her new home. "Yes, and quite large. Are you all staying in this unit?"

"I was hoping I could stay with you and Roger. I want to get to know you better and Roger is always good for a hoot."

"Yes, he is," Harry chuckled. "That would be great. You can use my bedroom and I'll go upstairs, into my old room. Roger has the downstairs guest room."

"Perhaps I should share with Roger. That would make for an interesting week." She laughed and blushed when she realized she may have shocked Harry. "I'm just joking. The upstairs room will be fine."

The handsome assistant, Jonathon, approached with the beautiful blonde Lila on his right and young Charlie on his left. "We're all set, Caroline," he chimed. "Do you want us to start with the digging?"

Harry cringed at the suggestion. He wanted to scream, but he couldn't. "I thought breakfast was in order. There is bacon and eggs in the pantry. If one of you would like to cook, we can eat, have coffee, and discuss the matter."

Caroline sensed Harry's reluctance to the concept of them exhuming the remains of his victims, so she agreed with him. "Yes, let's eat and discuss. Harry, lead the way. Charlie, get my suitcase from the motorhome and bring it into the house, would you?"

"Sure, Grandma."

Caroline hated that name. "It's Carol, Charlie. No need to be irritating in front of our host, OK?"

"Yes, Carol." There was a smirk on his face as he opened the door of the motorhome. "Am I staying in the house or here?"

"I was thinking you could camp out in the backyard with the graves. Someone has to watch over the dead."

Everyone laughed at the thought, except Charlie. "Not going to happen, Grandma." he snapped and climbed into the motorhome.

Harry ushered the group into the kitchen and showed Carol around the house while Roger talked to Jonathon and Lila, who organized the kitchen for breakfast. Roger sat at the table and looked through Harry's daily newspaper. There was an article about a rumor that the FBI was in Bad Axe, asking questions. He read the article with intent and put the paper in Jonathon's hand. "Check this out, John."

"Don't worry, Roger. Everything is under control. There won't be any problems."

Roger looked worried and turned as Harry and Carol returned from their exploration.

"Thank you, Harry." She walked to the kitchen window and looked over the backyard, with one hole dug next to the border. "So this is where you buried the bodies?"

Harry watched her and expected the question. "Yes."

"It's a beautiful backyard. Too bad we'll have to dig it all up." Harry cringed, and Carol watched him squirm. "Look, Harry. Roger has informed us about everything he has learned. We're here to clean up the mess and learn everything we can about what happened. Today we will study the bones from your first victim. Lila and I will analyze them, and Charlie and John will dig up the next one. In less than a week, we should have a better idea how they died."

"I understand, Carol. But that doesn't make it any easier."

"No, it doesn't. But if we can prove you didn't kill these sixteen people, that will alter your life." Carol watched her junior assistants at the stove cooking eggs, bacon, and hash-browns. "Lila, do you need me to make the toast?"

"No, Carol. I'll handle it, but tomorrow I might suggest having someone find the nearest McDonalds. Takeout would be easier."

Harry laughed. "There is a McDonalds a mile away. For lunch I suggest takeout pizza, and tonight we could go out for dinner."

After enjoying breakfast, the investigators went outside to begin preparations for their work. Carol asked Harry if he could stay back and help her make a list of the sixteen victims. "Roger says you remember each one. If you can describe them, as we exhume them we will compare your version with the forensic facts."

"I'm not sure whether Roger told you, I see their ghosts every day. Sometimes they try to talk to me; other times they just stand in the backyard watching." Harry watched Carol. He wanted to see her reaction, hoping it wasn't one of pity. That was not a reaction he wanted. She is an attractive, intelligent, available woman, and he doesn't want to ruin his chances with a pity card.

"I'm not surprised. I don't think I could have handled the situation if I were you. You've proven your strength of character. Even if you killed these people, you overcame the guilt by living a full life. Kathy told me a lot about you. She was proud of you, and I know she loved you, in her own way."

"You knew my wife?" He didn't know many of his wife's friends.

"Yes, in college, and then we were close friends after school. Kathy kept her friends close. I'm not sure why she didn't introduce us, perhaps because you were always busy on another trial. I watched your career, and I have to admit, you fascinate me. Such an intelligent man, but you never sought to go higher. Didn't you ever want to be a judge or hold public office?"

As the two talked, Harry sat with a pen and paper, writing the sixteen victims of his crime. "No," he replied to her question. "I didn't feel worthy of those positions. I became a lawyer so I could defend myself when I got caught."

Carol laughed. "Great idea. Let's try to avoid that."

Harry wrote the last name on his list and handed it to her. "If I could, I would take a photo of the ghosts I see and attach one to each person."

Carol read out loud the list which had the victim's numbers and gave their names and descriptions.

01 - (Casandra) Broken Girl. Nine years old girl, arm gone, head damaged.
02 - (Mary) Baby One. Unknown cause of death.
03 - (Marshall) Baby Two. Unknown cause of death.
04 - (Clara) Bad Axe Woman. Old lady, no sign of violence
05 - (William) Farmer Bill. Burned to death.
06 - (Clarence) Caseville Man. Head held under his arm.
07 - (Jimmy) Young man with a crushed skull.
08 - (Orville) Big Man in his mid-fifties with only one leg.
09 - (Anna) Fragile small woman, unknown cause of death.
10 - (Omar) Small man, mid-twenties, crushed head.
11 - (Allen) Child about five years old with no sign of violence.
12 - (Chester) Man around forty with no sign of violence.
13 - (Angela) Fifty-year-old woman with no sign of

violence.

14 - (Cora) Teenage girl with a bullet hole in her head.

15 - (Robert) Teenage boy with a hole in his head.

16 - (Arnold) Old man with unknown cause of death.

After reading the list, Carol turned away, wiped tears from her eyes, and sighed. "Harry, I want to end the pain that you are enduring. You can't carry this guilt for the rest of your life. I'm sorry, I have to go out and start my work." She didn't wait for his comment and hurried away.

Harry felt dejected and followed her outside. He watched her gather around her team as they read the list. They all looked back and saw him standing on the deck. He turned and walked to the door. Tears filled his eyes. Anna, his ninth victim, walked through the door after Harry and followed him to the table. He heard her speak for the first time. "Don't worry. It's OK."

CHAPTER 12

Roger approached Harry and sat down next to him at the table. "I want to do another hypnosis session."

"How will it help now? Carol's team is out digging up the whole backyard. I had to give her a list of the dead."

"Do you have a copy? I need to see it." Roger stood as Harry replied, "no."

"I'm going out to see it. Do you have a copy machine?" asked Roger

"Yes. What's so important about the list." Harry grew curious, but Roger didn't wait to give him an answer. He walked through the side door. Harry stood and watched him walk into the backyard, approach Carol, and remove the list from her clipboard. He ran back into the house. "Where is the copy machine? She wants this list back. Her team is digging on the second and third graves."

The two walked into the living room, and Harry took the list and made several copies. Roger ran the original back outside and returned to the kitchen, where Harry was warming up his coffee.

"So?" asked Roger. "Can we do the hypnosis session?"

"Why do you feel you need to ask? You didn't ask the first time," Harry goaded Roger.

"Because I want you to feel that you can trust me. I should have asked the first time, too."

"Be my guest. Pry into my brain and find the killer, but if he gets out and starts adding more bodies, it's all on you, Roger."

Roger let out a hesitant laugh. Harry was kidding, but the truth was there. If there is a killer in Harry's subconscious mind, he could overwhelm Harry and take control. It was a risk the doctor will take.

In a few minutes, Harry was under the spell... Relaxed-and ready to talk about the fourth burial.

The doctor plugged his web-cam into his laptop and made notes on the notebook. After adjusting the video and volume, he said, "Harry, we are going back to when you were almost eleven. There is a period that you may be blocking. Do you remember burying the three babies?"

"Yes. It was awful. The babies were so small. I cried all night. How could I have killed those little babies? It made me so angry with myself. So angry."

"Harry, go back to when you were nine years old. Tell me about your dad, the time he was angry at you."

After a few seconds, Harry's face grew grim. "Daddy doesn't love me. He yells at me and sometimes he hits me. I don't remember what happened."

"Harry, you are sleepy. Relax... You can remember. You are with your dad. Push through the haze. You will remember. Tell me what's happening."

"I was crying and Daddy slapped me and told me to stop being a baby. But Daddy, I did nothing wrong. He tried to touch me. Mommy said I should tell you. She said you would tell him to leave me alone."

"Who touched you, Harry?" Roger asked.

"Daddy's boss. He put his hand down my pants. I didn't like that, and I told him to stop. He said Dad would lose his job if I didn't let him play with it. I asked Daddy, *will you lose your job because I ran away from your boss?* I don't want to talk about this. Please stop. I remember nothing else." Harry began sobbing.

"Harry, you are very relaxed. Open your eyes."

Harry smiled. "See, there wasn't anything new, was there?"

"Nothing new. Let's take a walk outside, then we can continue when we get back. OK?"

The doctor tried to be upbeat, but the revelation of Harry's abuse filled his mind with more questions. Did the abuse continue? Did Harry succumb to the farmer's advances? Did Harry fabricate another personality to deal with the feelings of humiliation and shame? Is Farmer Bill the man who abused him?

The two men walked into the backyard. Charlie was working on grave number two, while Jonathon dug the third. Caroline and Lila were not outside. Roger yelled, "Jonathon, where are the women?"

"They're in the lab. I guess the two of us are going to be the general labor while they get the good jobs."

Charlie laughed, jumped out of the grave he had dug, and walked toward the three men. "Tell me, what am I learning by digging this old fart's graves up?"

Jonathon grabbed Charlie's arm and warned, "None of that attitude around here, kid. You treat him with respect, understood?"

"Yes, Sir. Sorry, Harry. It's been difficult working here. This place creeps me out." He looked around the yard, with the remaining fifteen white crosses standing like soldiers protecting their secrets.

Harry smiled. "Charlie, I can relate to that feeling. Have you reached the baby yet?"

"Yes, I was ready to stop when you guys showed up. I just unearthed what looked like tiny bones and the remains of clothing and a box. I need to get Grandma to come and look." Charlie turned toward Harry, looked into his eyes, and asked, "Did you kill all these people, Sir?"

Roger interrupted Harry's reply. "Charlie, that is why we are here. To find out what happened."

Harry interjected, "Yes., when I was young, I remember burying people."

"Awesome!" Charlie beamed with admiration and added, "You killed them, didn't you? Wow."

Harry didn't answer. He turned and let his eyes scan the backyard. It was odd that none of the ghosts were there. In fact, since the forensic team arrived, he has seen none of the ghosts, except Anna, the frail small woman, his ninth victim, who was abused and broken. *She came to me in the house to comfort me.* There was a stillness in the air, an ominous feeling of impending danger. He shook his arms, as if to cast off the feeling, but it remained.

Jonathon put his hand on Harry's shoulder. "Sir, are you OK? You looked a little dazed there."

"I'm fine. So what is your opinion of this crazy mess?" Harry asked in all seriousness. He doubted the process that Roger arranged. These four strangers are digging into his past, as if they discovered an Egyptian site.

Roger didn't let Jonathon reply. He interjected, "Harry, we're doing what has to be done. If we want to know how and why these graves are here, we have to dig them up, and I have brought in the best people to do that."

Jonathon agreed. "That's correct, Harry. We will treat this with all the respect it deserves. I still question how you, as a teenager, could have committed these atrocities."

CHAPTER 13

Caroline and Lila walked across the lawn, followed by Charlie. Lila yelled, "Jonathon, are both of the graves ready for us?"

"Yes, Lilly. Charlie and I dug down to the first sign of the bones. Now it's your grave."

Caroline studied the two graves and slid into the second one. "Lila, can you get down there, or do you need a ladder?"

Annoyed, Lila chimed, "No problem. I may be small, but I'm capable of jumping in and out of a grave, Carol."

While Carol and Lila worked in the graves, meticulously uncovering the bones, recording every aspect of their placement, and moving them into a plastic container to bring to the surface, Jonathon and Charlie took turns digging the fourth grave. Harry and Roger pulled the patio furniture closer to the gravesites.

Harry kept looking into the woods, wondering what happened to the ghosts. He told Roger. "Something strange is happening, Doctor. I only saw one ghost since Carol and her team arrived. Is that a good, or bad sign?"

Roger looked around the backyard and replied, "Well... what do you think?"

"I think you should stop turning things around. You tell me first!"

In his mind, Roger said, *perhaps you are accepting the reality of the moment.* The words that he uttered were, "I don't know, Harry. I never saw them, and I don't know why they stopped appearing for you."

Harry accepted Roger's reasoning. "I'm getting a beer. Do you want anything?"

"Yes! The other day, I put some in the refrigerator in your garage. You can bring me one and take one for yourself. Carol, anyone for a beer?" Roger yelled.

Carol placed the plastic container of bones on the edge of the grave and jumped out. "Yes, I could use an ice tea if you have one."

Roger laughed as everyone started giving him their drink orders at once. "I'm not the barmaid. Charlie, come help me."

The two walked into the garage as the team members found a seat on the patio. It was a beautiful day with bright sunshine, and Harry felt a healing sensation as the warm sun bathed him in comfort.

Lila sat down next to him. "Harry, you don't look like a killer. You're too kind. Most killers have an empty look in their eyes, but your eyes express joy, hope, and warmth."

"Thank you, Lila. Sometimes I wonder what is real and unreal. I can't imagine myself killing that innocent baby."

Roger and Charlie set the drinks on the table. "Well, Harry, I guess you and I are the only drinkers around here."

Carol laughed. "When we have work to get done, we can't afford to fog our minds. That will come tonight after work."

"Grandma, does that mean I can have a beer tonight, too?" Charlie asked, knowing the answer.

"Root beer, perhaps." Carol and her grandson have an understanding. He can do most anything he wants.

Harry explained to Charlie, "It started when I was ten, and I buried the last one while I was your age... still in high school."

"What do the ghosts look like? Are they transparent?"

"They look like misty figures, but they are solid. Sometimes they talk, and I can hear them. Other times, they talk without sound. I know they are talking, but it's silent. Perhaps I just don't listen. When I was in college, the dreams and ghosts disappeared. They only showed themselves when I came back to this property."

"Awesome. I hope I'll be able to see them. Perhaps if I try real hard, I will. Sometimes I see ghosts other people don't. Figures in a dark corner. You know, fleeting images that are hard to make out. Sometimes Grandma calls me her little psychic. I guess I'm sensitive to the paranormal."

"I wouldn't want anyone to see the poor souls I buried. It's bad enough that I see them."

"Are they here now?"

"No. They don't want to come out with you guys in the yard. Perhaps you frighten them!"

"Awesome. Harry, I hope you didn't kill them because I like you. You have a good aura around you."

Harry laughed. "And you can see my aura?"

"Yes, just like you can see your ghosts."

"Understood. I like you too, Charlie. You're not the little bastard that I was when I was your age."

Charlie stood, chuckling. "And I didn't kill sixteen people, either."

Roger was listening to the last of Charlie's and Harry's conversation. "Charlie, I'm sure Harry didn't kill sixteen people, either."

Harry looked stunned. "Where does that opinion come from, Roger?"

"From Caroline and Lila's observations of the bones. They are stymied. Your identifications have been very accurate. But the facts don't jive. There is no way a child of ten could have dug these graves. They are close to three feet deep. If you could dig them, why didn't your parents question the pile of dirt left behind. Graves are messy, Harry. It takes a long time for the soil to compact down. It makes little sense, but we'll figure it out."

Dumbfound, Harry replied, "With all my soul I know I buried them. I know who they are, I know what they look like, and I remember burying them. If I didn't put them in those graves, then who did?"

CHAPTER 14

Roger didn't have any answers to Harry's questions. Someone buried the sixteen bodies in his backyard, but he couldn't venture a guess who it was.

"Harry, I'm sorry. We will find out what the hell is going on here. I promise. We will study every grave for clues. You must trust that Caroline and Lila will find some answers. I just know you could not have buried them."

Harry stood and walked to the fourth grave where Jonathon and Charlie were taking turns shoveling dirt out of the grave. He knew they were close because all he could see was Jonathon's head and shoulders.

"Charlie, the woman in this grave is old and cantankerous. She often yells at me when I come into the yard. She and Farmer Bill must have known each other because they always show up together, and I buried them the same year."

Charlie laughed. "No ghost has risen from the grave yet. I have been getting some strange sensations while I dig, though. It's a chill that rises from the ground, and I've been hearing whispers and someone is crying in the woods. Do you see or hear any ghosts, now?"

"No. I think they are avoiding you and the team. Since you showed up, they have been hiding."

"Perhaps they don't like strangers. Let me know when you see one. I have a special camera and microphone that I would like to use."

"Do you believe in ghosts?" he asked.

"Of course I do. Didn't Roger tell you I have been studying the paranormal? Grandma and I both have seen ghosts at our work. Sometimes when a person dies, they leave energy behind, in the bones. Grandma thinks it's that energy that manifests itself as a ghost."

"Wow. I'm surprised, and I guess a little pleased. Thanks for telling me that."

Charlie looked into the grave. "John, you ready for me to dig?"

Jonathon's head peeked over the edge of the grave. "Yes, I just uncovered the foot. Tell Carol she can work on this one."

Harry tried to get close to the edge of the old woman's grave, but Jonathon scurried him away. "Sir, we can't have you too close to the scene... of a...." His words stumbled and Harry noticed.

"Scene of the crime? Is that what you were going to say? Jonathon, you're more than Carol's assistant, aren't you?"

"Yes. I am an FBI specialist. I wanted to tell you up front, but Roger was afraid it would push you over the edge. We are investigating this incident as a potential crime. We don't want to have a circus, so we work undercover. The local and state police are aware of our operations."

"And Caroline? Is she undercover?" Harry bit back.

"Well, I don't know how she is under the covers, but I know Lilly does a marvellous job." Jonathon broke out laughing. "No, she's Carol. When we have a case with paranormal issues, we bring Caroline, Lilly and Charlie to help. They're the best!"

Harry worked his way to the patio and slumped into a chair. His head was spinning out of control, and he felt like his feet were going to sink into the earth. He thought, *so this is the way it's going to go down. Damn... Well, what did I expect. I'm a fucking lawyer. I knew better than...*

"Harry," Jonathon called, and sat next to him. "I want you to look forward to our ability to prove you never killed these people. I don't know what's going on here, but the facts don't add up. And when the evidence says no, the no's have it."

Harry adjusted and stretched his back and stood. "I'm going in for another beer. I'd get you one, but according to Carol you don't drink?"

"My work is done, so you can bring me one too."

When Harry returned with a large bucket of cold beer and ice, the entire team greeted him. Carol and Jonathon were talking, while Charlie and Lilly sat on the grass chatting. Harry thought, *one second this was a place of doom, and the next it's a happy family enjoying the outdoors in the backyard. And only twelve more victims to be exhumed.*

Roger walked out of the kitchen, holding a mixed drink. "Harry, isn't this nice? Beautiful summer afternoon, friends, and cold drinks. This is excellent therapy for you."

Harry wasn't listening. He was watching Carol and Jonathon talk. *She, a little angry, tried to calm her. She pulled away from the grip he had on her arm, she slapped him and kicked him in the groin.* Harry blinked and realized he was daydreaming. "Hey, Doctor, any chance I could go nuts before I go to trial. I might need a good defense strategy?"

"Stop talking like that, Harry. That's crazy talk, and you are far from crazy. Old and crotchety, yes, but not crazy."

"OK. No crazy talk, but I just noticed Clara, the old lady you dug up, and Farmer Bill standing in the woods, over there." Harry pointed, and everyone followed his finger into the wooded area. Nothing. "They backed away when they saw you looking at them. Charlie, did you see anything?"

"No, sorry Sir. My eyes were on the lovely Lilly, not the ghosts."

Lila pushed him, "Stop that."

Carol laughed, "Yes, Charlie, she is lovely. Don't touch."

Jonathon and Carol approached Harry. Carol smiled and

said, "We need to talk. There are revelations we need to discuss. I ordered several pizzas delivered tonight, so we have about an hour to show you the evidence we have uncovered and determine where we are going from here."

Harry gave a nod of agreement and said, "Do you want this to be a private or group discussion?"

Carol, in a get-your-attention voice, yelled, "Everyone around the table. We're having a meeting now."

The chairs were slid around on the concrete and when silence filled the air, Carol began, "Harry knows that we are conducting a criminal investigation. He guessed it, and we could see no reason to lie. Lila and I confirmed that the bones of the first four victims are old and meet Harry's description. We need to send samples for a positive date."

She took a deep breath and added, "Ever since Harry was ten years old, he's known the bones were there, and who the victims were. Did he take part in their deaths? Did he bury the bodies, as he's believed since he was a child? These are the questions; we have none answered."

CHAPTER 15

The pizza arrived with two large salads. After dinner, the team went into Harry's home to listen to music and enjoy their first evening at the graveyard. To Harry's relief, the conversation did not focus on him. The team talked about some of their more troublesome cases. A serial killer who spread the body parts across the country, unidentified bones found in the woods south of Ann Arbor, and a B&B up north with ghosts disrupting the visitors.

"That last one was special," Carol told Harry. "We found the bones in the basement and helped set the woman free. It started one hundred years ago when her husband killed her and buried her beneath the floor. She wanted someone to find her, and we did."

Harry considered his situation... something that was second nature to him as he is always trying to figure out the why of his life. "The ghosts here don't want us to find them. They're afraid to leave. That's why they're angry now... you are moving them away from their home and family group."

Charlie added, "There are several reasons souls can't move on, having a violent death, or not wanting to leave a loved one. I think some poor souls just get lost and can't find their way in the darkness."

Carol was beaming at her grandson. "Clever, Charlie. But why haven't you seen any ghosts here?"

Harry nodded his head. "I think it's because they know he will see them. That's why they are hiding. In time I think you'll see them, Charlie. I am positive they are real and not figments of my imagination."

Roger was at the kitchen table, working on his laptop. Harry didn't realize it, but Roger set up a slew of Wi-Fi video cameras in the home and yard. He was monitoring the camera in the backyard and noticed a hazy figure walking up to another hazy figure. "Harry, get over here, NOW," he yelled.

Harry jumped up and hurried to Roger's side. "What's so important?"

The other members of the team followed him. Roger pointed to the video and said, "There was a cloudy area and I thought it might have been a ghost."

Jonathon interjected, "Roger, there isn't anything there. Why don't you check the recording? You recorded it, didn't you?"

"No, I only record when I'm working with Harry, to watch his progress. I expected nothing to happen that I would want recorded. Sorry." Roger closed the laptop.

Harry's mind fogged for a moment; then he realized what they announced. "Roger, when did you put these cameras up, where are they, and why did you invade my privacy like this?"

"I did them the first day I arrived. You had some indoor work to do, so I went outdoors; then after you went to bed, I put the indoor cameras up. They do not cover the bathrooms, bedrooms, or upstairs. The basement is camera-free also, but there are two outdoor cameras covering the backyard."

Carol approached Roger and Harry. "Guys. It's been a tense day. I think we all could use some rest. In the morning I want to dig the remains of six more victims."

Roger cringed at that word. "Carol, stop calling them victims. We don't know what happened to them. I am sure Harry didn't kill them."

Jonathon walked over to the laptop and lifted the monitor. "Roger, I will set this up so the cameras will upload to the FBI cloud storage drive. They will be secure and, Harry, I'll set a password so only we can access them. If there is something paranormal happening here, we need it recorded."

"Excellent idea, John." Lila cooed as she approached him. She ran her hand down his back, bent down to whisper in his ear, cupped his cheek, and smiled as he squirmed. "How long will you be working on this computer thing? I'm thinking of going back to the motorhome. If you're late, wake me... OK?"

"Will do, and I'll work faster knowing."

She squeezed a little harder and walked away. "Charlie, you coming with me?"

"Later. I want to talk to Harry before I go back." Charlie was watching Jonathon set up the cameras so they would record twenty-four-seven. He set the image size small enough that the digital files wouldn't be too huge. "John, will we be able to see outside in the dark?"

"No, these are cheap cameras." Jonathon turned to Harry. "OK if we keep the outside lights on? That way we aren't walking in the dark and we'll have light to record."

"That's fine. Did everyone hear that?" Harry's voice grew louder. "Don't turn the outdoor lights off."

Jonathon added, "Indoors won't be a problem because... Harry is afraid of the dark, and has a zillion little lights all over the place."

His head down, Harry said, "If you lived my life, the darkness would hold fear for you, too."

CHAPTER 16

When Jonathon arrived at the motorhome, Lila was in the kitchen mixing a rum and coke. "Do you want one? We can bring them into the bedroom."

"What about Charlie? He'll be coming back soon. If he doesn't see me, he'll know we're together."

Lila laughed. "Charlie knows, he's smarter than both of us together. Just leave a *Do Not Disturb* sign on the counter."

She put her arms behind his neck and pulled him to her waiting lips. He rubbed against her as they kissed. "Charlie doesn't need a sign," he mumbled as she led him to the bedroom. He stopped to clean up and found her naked on the bed. Dropping clothing as he moved, he lay beside her. She took control, led him, controlled his movements and passion, making sure he satisfied her first.

"Your turn." she slid down, inch by inch, her tongue tasting and teasing its way down to the goal of her quest. He gasped. She brought him to the finish line... stopped and said, "Do you want me, now?" He leaped into action, lifting her into a comfortable position for his invasion. He found the target and aimed his energized and throbbing missile.

"Yes... deeper... deeper... harder... faster... oh God... yes... yes... yes."

Charlie heard the last yes. He smiled and thought, *Good job, John Boy. I should be so lucky.* He slid his hand into his jeans, rubbed, and checked his phone. *Aha. My lucky night too... I have Wi-Fi.*

Harry spent the evening awake in bed, thinking about the past few weeks. Outside he heard an owl and the rustling of a raccoon trying to get into the trash can. *Life goes on,* he thought. *I wonder if I'll end up in jail, or a mental ward in some lonely hospital. It would be easier if I were dead, like Farmer Bill and the rest of them. Perhaps that's what they want, me joining them in the graveyard.*

Carol knocked on his door and asked, "Are you sleeping, Harry?"

"No. The door is open."

She walked into the dimmed room. "I had to use the bathroom and wanted to talk to you, alone. Is that OK?"

"Yes." He sat up and slid so his back was against the headboard. "Come, have a seat next to me."

Carol smiled, "I'll be back in a second," and scurried out of the room. Harry heard her in the kitchen, and when she returned, she placed a half bottle of wine and two glasses on the nightstand. She sat beside him, filled both glasses, and handed him one.

"Now, isn't this better?"

"Yes, this is nice." Harry sipped the sweet red wine and placed it on his night stand. "What is it you wanted to talk about?"

"There are some things you should know. You are aware I knew your wife. We went through college together and were close... very close... intimate. She never told you or anyone other than her female friends about her other side."

Harry didn't speak. Images filled his mind as he traced his married life back to when he first met his wife, Kathy.

Carol studied his face. "Harry. Do you understand what I'm saying?"

"Trust me Carol, I understand." He took another sip of wine, smiled, and took a deep breath. "I'm amazed at Kathy's ability to live two lives... she was creative... like I was."

"Yes. Kathy made her life a game, loving the ability to manipulate other people, and she was skilled."

"I admit, I suspected. I mean, a woman can have only so many female friends... right?"

"Perhaps. Either way, your wife was a fantastic woman, wasn't she?"

Harry laughed. "Yes, Carol. Kathy was a fantastic woman, but her love could not be bound to one person. I knew it, but it made it easy for me to hide from my past. For my goals in life, we made the ideal couple."

Carol's laughter almost caused her wine glass to topple to the floor.

"Harry, I sure hope you're not a killer, because I could fall for you... not as a victim, but as a friend or lover."

"Same here, I can see why Kathy was into you." He gripped her hand and smiled. "I too, hope I didn't kill those people."

Carol stood, gathered the wine and glasses, turned, and said, "Harry, I will find the truth. Something tells me it won't be all your fault." She shut the door before he could reply.

Harry heard her climb the stairs and walk to the bedroom he once... *God, so many (once did) moments. If I'm not guilty of killing them, and I didn't bury them, what the fuck did I do to deserve this HELL?*

***

The night was still. In the graveyard, a gathering of the souls started. Farmer Bill and the Bad Axe woman walk around calling for a rising. The old woman whispers, "Rise my family, rise and help us save our world. Rise my children. The time has come."

One by one, hands reach up, grabbing a shaft of air, pulling the mist from the grave. Young Casandra's one arm wipes the sleep from her eye. "What's happening? Grandma, what are we doing up?" she watched as the others gathered around Grandma, the Bad Axe woman.

"My friends and children, we must stop these invaders tonight. Honey, give me your hand. Bill, put your hand on her shoulder, touch the one next to you. Amplify our voice, for tonight we sing."

It started as a whispered hymn. A prayer sung by the old woman. One by one they joined her in their praise and glory, as the old man Arnold began an incantation. Sounding like a preacher, he spoke, "*Spirits of the underworld, listen to my holy words. We are family, we are one with the earth, ties that cannot be broken bind our souls to this land. Let us destroy those who would cut our chains of love. Together we can… and will destroy the invaders. We will survive as a family for eternity.*"

Grandma continued singing her hymn, and the family of spirits raised their voices in unison. "*Praise HE who has given us hope and joy, praise him and adore him, for HE is the ONE.*"

Charlie stirred in bed and listened to the sound. He pulled the curtains back and saw fog moving in from the woods. Standing at the window, he slipped on his underwear and went to the door. One thought ran through his mind, *I should wake John and Lila;* he didn't.

Grabbing the LED torch next to the door, he stepped outside. In the chilled wind he could hear the sounds of a church choir. He flashed the light into the woods and felt a burning chill and a sharp pain hit him in the chest. Something passed through his body. He fell to his knees, his hands holding his chest and his head on the ground.

What the hell was that? Before he could get up, the entire choir of ghosts passed through his mind and body. He screamed at the top of his young lungs and collapsed, face down, into the lawn.

CHAPTER 17

*B*y *the time everyone was in the backyard, Charlie was awake and sitting on the grass.*

Jonathon rushed into Harry's home as Carol sat next to Charlie. "What happened?"

"I think a gang of ghosts raped me."

Roger looked at Harry. "I thought ghosts couldn't hurt you. What is he talking about?"

Charlie overheard the question and said, "They ran through me. Their energy tore me a new one, so to speak."

"Odd, they never did that to me." Harry helped Carol stand and continued. "Tell me, Charlie, why did you come outside?"

"I heard singing. I think the old lady was leading the ghosts in a hymn."

"Did you see them?" Harry asked.

"Not at first... when I did, they gored me. The first time one ghost stunned me, then they hit with full force. I still ache, inside." He rubbed his abdomen and shivered. "I swear all of them passed through me, like light streaming through a window."

Jonathon returned from Harry's house. "I checked the recording, it shows Charlie getting hit, but nothing else. It's like he's a mime reacting to unseen forces. I'll show you it in the morning. Is Charlie going to be OK?" he asked.

"Yes. I'm fine," Charlie said. "Let's go back to bed. I'll feel better in the morning." He thanked Carol and Harry and followed Lila and Jonathon into the motorhome. "It sounded like the two of you were doing fine last night, too."

Jonathon turned quickly, "Kid, don't go there."

"OK. Don't make all those sex sounds, then. OK?"

Lila whispered in his ear, "You're just jealous, because the only penetration you got was with a ghost. Was it exciting? I bet they took your virginity, didn't they?"

"Shut up, Lila." Charlie walked to his bed and collapsed on his back. "I lost that long ago."

Lila was ready to add another insult, but Jonathon stopped her. "That's enough, let's go back to bed."

"You can sleep out here, John. I need my beauty sleep." She shut the bedroom door.

"Well, kid, I guess it's you and me."

"Don't get any stupid ideas, John."

"Shut up and go to sleep. If you decide to run outside again... well... don't."

***

The sun streamed into the motorhome, awakening both Charlie and Jonathon. Charlie was first in the bathroom. "Don't take all morning, Charlie," Jonathon warned. "I have to pee too."

Lila walked out in a short, pink robe. "What's going on? You guys sounded like a stampede of horses."

Jonathon gave her a quick kiss. "Charlie was first to the bathroom. I'm going outside to piss."

"Don't piss on the graves. They won't like that if you do."

"Shut up, Lila."

Charlie walked out of the bathroom as Lila walked in for her shower. He noticed Jonathon standing in the yard. He watched him for a few moments, then looked into the woods. *I better not encounter them again today.* He cleaned his area, organized the kitchen... as his mind kept going back to the pain he felt last night.

Lila stepped into the kitchen. Her hair was wet, and she had a large towel around her. "I'm done in the bathroom. Jonathan forgot to connect the water hose, so you could run out."

Charlie wasn't listening. He turned around, saw her, and grabbed his jeans and a clean shirt.

As he walked to the bathroom he said, "Call Grandma and ask if we are going to Harry's for breakfast." The door closed and Jonathon returned, saw the bathroom door shut, and knew he missed his turn again.

Lila made the call to Carol and yelled back to Charlie, "We're going to Harry's for breakfast. Roger is picking up McDonalds. What do you want?"

"The big breakfast. I'm sure Harry will have coffee."

Lila placed their orders, and Carol said it would be about forty-five minutes.

Jonathon grabbed his jeans, pulled them on, and flexed his bare chest. Lila noticed and smiled.

"Looks like I'm not taking a shower unless I hook up the hose to this place. Too bad we don't have sewer nearby." He walked toward the door, but Lila stopped him with her arm. Hold on, tiger. She ran her hand down his unbuttoned jeans. "I just needed a touch to keep me thinking about the fun it's been, so far."

Jonathon pulled her hand out. "Be sure to wash that hand; you never know where it's been… and yes it's been fun, so far." He stepped out and around the side of the motorhome, where he found a retractable hose. He pulled it toward Harry's garage and fell short about twenty-five feet.

After rooting around in the garage, he returned with a garden hose. A few connections later, and the Mobile Palace of Sin had water… to clean the *living*.

Jonathon returned. "We have running water, so I can take my shower."

A KILLER WITHIN

Looking refreshed, Charlie... wearing tight stretch jeans, grabbed his black hooded sweatshirt and opened the door. "The bathroom is all yours. I'm looking around outside and I'll try not to get raped by the ghosts again."

Lila laughed, "Have fun. If you like, you can start on grave number five." She picked up her copy of Harry's list, "Ah yes, you might like him. It's Farmer Bill. Harry burned him to death. Be careful Charlie; don't bend over while you're digging him out."

"You know Lila, for a brilliant forensic expert, you can be very crass."

Jonathon listened to the conversations from the bathroom. He stuck his head out the door and said, "Lila, he's got you pegged."

"Shut up, John."

Lila grabbed a glass of water and studied the list of victims. She tried to picture a pattern. *None.* Looking through her notes on the bones she studied yesterday, she thought, *Nothing here either. Odd. The pieces of fabric we found and the boxes (or caskets) all seem too planned. The little girl had a doll in her grave. And a cross. Someone placed her in the grave with love and sorrow. Is this something a young boy would do? Not the boys I knew when I was a child.*

CHAPTER 18

Roger and Carol returned from McDonalds. The team walked together into Harry's kitchen. Roger put the containers down and announced, "Pick out what you want. I ordered extra, just in case."

There was a mad dash to grab the food orders. Carol stood and yelled, "Children, slow down. We have a lot to do today, so conserve that exuberant energy."

Roger chuckled to himself, and Carol asked, "Well, tell us what's so funny, Mr. Psychiatrist."

Roger blushed; he did not plan to tell everyone his thoughts. "Their exuberant energy is sexual tension and anxiety working together to push their minds into a competitive state, leading to risk taking."

Charlie smiled and riffed, "Impressive, Doc. But Lilly Budd is the oversexed tease, if you please, and Jonathon always has something up his sleeve."

"What the fuck are you talking about, kid?" Jonathon insisted.

Lila stretched her head around and added, "Yeah. What do you mean?"

Carol put her arm around her grandson. "Guys, remember, Charlie is special. It's difficult for him to control his thoughts, or perhaps he just likes to be the mirror in the room."

"Grandma, don't call me special!"

Charlie grabbed his coffee and a big breakfast and walked into the living room. *I'm miles ahead of those idiots,* he thought.

I just need to decide who I'm competing against and for.

Harry announced, "I need your attention. I called a rental dealer and arranged the delivery of a small backhoe. It has a bucket and can dig dirt from a hole. Does anyone here know how to run one? If we don't have someone, I need to call Bob and have him send someone. Not sure you want a stranger in your midst."

Jonathon raised his arm, holding an egg sandwich. "I ran a bobcat in the Army. Of course that was ten years ago, but I'm sure I can figure it out."

"Great," replied Carol. "After breakfast, you guys should be able to get at least four more of the graves excavated."

***

Roger took his coffee and breakfast into the living room. He sat down next to Charlie. "How are you feeling after last night's trauma?"

It relieved Charlie that someone asked. "I'm fine." He gave his quick answer, the one always on the tip of his tongue. With thought, he shared with the good doctor, Roger.

"You know, Doc, I've had plenty of experiences with ghosts. This is the first time they assaulted me. Harry's victims aren't angry at him; they don't want to lose him. We are the invaders of their world. The question I have now is, did Harry's assault create the ghosts-or-did the ghosts assault Harry and pull him into theirs?"

A broad grin appeared on the good doctor's face as he realized his observations were also those of someone he admired. "Yes, Charlie, you are wise again. Keep it up, son. You will make it... as you learn. But I was talking about you. If *you* have something you want to share, I'm here to listen and perhaps give guidance. I see how Lila and Jonathon tease you. Doesn't that bother you?"

"Hell no... well... perhaps on one level. Like I said, Lila is a tease. I first met her two years ago, when I was fifteen and had just received my high school diploma. Grandma hired her as an assistant. Lila grew up with three brothers and now she treats her men like toys. Sex toys, if you will. I can handle her teasing and sexual innuendos, and of course I wouldn't turn down a genuine offer. I mean, she is *hot* for an old woman."

"Thirty-five is not old," Roger retorted.

"Not to you, but to me... she's old. Sexy, but still old."

"What about Jonathon?" The doctor had noticed the tension between the two and took notice of Charlie's comment. "You said Jonathon has something up his sleeve. Tell me what you mean by that."

"He's an enigma." Charlie smiled. "I like him, but he can be a military asshole. Which reminds me, I have to get out there and help John Boy... dig a hole... to another soul."

Charlie hurried out of the room and Roger stood, seeing Harry sitting in the chair next to him.

"Harry, you startled me. Are you doing OK? No dreams last night, besides Carol's gang of misfits and fiends?"

Harry laughed. "Misfits and fiends? You meant mystics and friends, didn't you?"

"Of course. Charlie can be quite a challenge, can't he." Roger sat down, taking the *doctor* roll again. "Don't you find it amazing that Charlie is so much like you were, when you were his age?"

"SHIT, ROGER. Don't tell me I'm hypnotized in your office, and none of this is happening, now. God, Roger... That would be cruel punishment!"

"no... No... NO... I am here in your house. The team is digging the graves with the new toy dig-err-thing, and you are here with me. I just observed that Charlie is a lot like you were as a teen. Perhaps we can, through him and the team, put your demons to rest."

Every bone in Harry's body went limp when he thought this moment could be another dream or hypnosis session. He stood and turned to Roger. "We should get outside. I'm not sure Jonathon can handle the heavy equipment, and I wouldn't want him getting hurt."

As the two men walked through the kitchen, Roger grabbed another sandwich from the table. "We should put these away so they don't spoil." He threw the remaining food in a takeout bag and tossed it into the refrigerator.

"Trust me, Roger; someone will eat them before lunch."

The cool morning breeze felt wonderful. The delivery man parked his trailer in the driveway, and the entire team watched as he unloaded the backhoe. Harry approached the backhoe, and as the delivery man stepped off the machine, Harry asked, "Are you Albert?"

The middle aged man nodded. "That's me."

"Your boss said you could show my man how to use the backhoe on this machine."

Jonathon approached. "Harry, I'll take care of this. You can go to the side and watch. I got it."

Albert began, "This is the key, and these are your..."

Jonathon interrupted. "Let's save time. It all looks familiar, so you can go. I got it from here."

The driver raised his trailer and handed Harry the invoice. "Call us when you want it picked up. And good luck, Sir."

It took Jonathon five minutes to figure out how to start the backhoe, and by the time he was digging, everyone except Charlie was back, working on their other tasks.

"Harry," Roger interrupted, "We need to have another session. Our sessions are bringing us closer to finding out when your dream reality problem began. I want to go back to when you talked to your father about his boss's attempted abuse of you."

Harry couldn't protest; he was under the good doctor's spell, in a deep sleep. In a trance like state, he watched as events passed within his mind's eye.

CHAPTER 19

The doctor turned on his light, adjusted the camera and microphone. "Harry, you are resting, alone in your room. Go back to when you told your dad about his boss touching you."

"I don't want to." Harry fidgeted in his seat. "I don't remember."

There was a long pause, "Nothing, nothing happened."

In a pleading, child-like voice, Harry said, "Please don't make me. I can't."

"Harry, relax. The truth can't hurt you. It is now past." The doctor touched Harry's shoulder with the kindness that the nine-year-old Harry needed.

"You know, when the farmer touched me, it was like electricity exploding. Is that bad? It scared me and I knew it was wrong. That's why I told him to stop and I ran away. I didn't want it to happen. I mean, I wanted it, but not from him. I always dreamed my best friend, Judy, would touch me that way."

"Harry, tell me again what your dad said. You can remember; it won't hurt to utter the words."

"He was yelling at me. He said, you little fag, why did you act that way with my boss."

"But, daddy, I didn't do it. He did."

"The way you act; all the men think you're a little sissy. Stop acting like a sissy and my boss will leave you alone. He thinks you're asking for it, you little fag." Tears ran down Harry's cheeks.

Roger held Harry's hands. "Son, your dad was wrong. He was very wrong to tell you that. I'm sorry, Harry. You are asleep, deeply asleep. When you awaken, you will remember what your father did and said. You will feel a great weight lifted from your heart. Wake up, Harry."

Harry opened his eyes as tears continued. "Did I create an alter personality? Is that who the killer is?" he asked.

"I'm not sure. If you created another personality, it would have happened at that moment."

Roger sipped his coffee and turned the recording off. "We still don't know why you started burying the dead. If it was a figment of your imagination, I could see. The reality is... we have real bones and ghosts. I want to help you. Charlie told me this morning that he wants to help them find their way home."

Roger continued, "We are ending with ever more questions, and these questions all have to be answered."

Harry wasn't listening. He visualized the look on his father's face. It was one of hate and loathing. *Why did Dad hold such animosity towards me? Was there something wrong with him? With me? He never liked me, and I always knew that. Then he never liked Mom, either. It wasn't until after he retired that he became a kinder man, it was too late... he died, without ever...*

Harry broke off his thought, stood, and walked to the door. After watching Charlie and Jonathon, he turned and said, "Well, Roger, that puts a whole new light on the situation, doesn't it?"

"Yes. We have to up the wattage. The light has to be strong before we can see the whole truth."

"I think I understand what you mean, but right now I want a beer, but it's too early in the day."

"You have my approval. I'll have a scotch and water, no ice."

The two sipped their drinks. Roger liked Harry. He saw a

man who suffered all his life, yet remained kind and understanding. *Harry could have embraced the evil and continued until his death. Perhaps he is the victim. Perhaps Charlie is correct in asking if the ghosts are the evil ones here. Did they attack the young boy? That would mean they were here first.*

Harry walked out the door, alone.

The good doctor had more work to do. He opened his computer to search for clues. *Perhaps I need to find the previous owners. What if someone else killed these people and made Harry bury them? What if it was Harry's dad? Or more likely there is another personality, hiding inside Harry's subconscious mind... ready to take control again.*

As Roger read through his notes and watched Harry's recordings... his mind slid back to his own life... to his dad, and the day he told him he was gay. The *look* in his dad's eyes, the *disappointment*, then the utter *sadness*. It took years before he felt loved again... that glorious day when his dad walked up to him. "I'm sorry, Roger."

"What for, Dad?"

"For thinking of myself, instead of you. For caring more about what my friends would say, than how you feel. For not being there while you suffered... alone. I'm sorry, and I love you... as you are."

Roger stopped. Closed his laptop and took the last sip in his glass. He sat the glass in the sink, looked out the window at the crew working, and sighed. Being involved in something this amazing wasn't what he expected when Harry walked into his office. *Hard to believe one man could hold so many secrets and still have more secrets to be unearthed.*

He walked through the door toward the graveyard.

CHAPTER 20

Harry walked around the holes in his yard and watched Jonathon manipulate the bucket, scooping and piling dirt next to the grave.

"I'm impressed," he yelled to Jonathon.

Roger approached the portable forensic laboratory. "Carol, can I come in?"

Carol stood at the door. "It's too small and crowded; I'll come out for a minute."

Roger stepped down and watched Carol approach him.

"Roger, we need to talk about Harry and these bones."

Together, they walked to the patio table. Roger went into the garage and returned with two Cokes. "How are you doing with your analysis of the bones?" he asked.

"That's what I want to talk about. I sent a bone sample of the little girl with only one arm to the University lab for dating." Carol stopped to sip her drink. "They called with the results." She took another sip, taking her time to reveal the information.

Roger became agitated. "Don't drag this out forever, Carol. I know you like the dramatic, but what do you know?"

"Hold on to your panties, Roger. You're always twisting them into a bunch. Now, as I was saying. I received the preliminary results, and along with the evidence we found with the bones... clothing (material, style, and construction), buttons (material used and style), and the religious artifacts, I have determined that Harry could not have killed or buried these people."

"Why not?" Roger asked. His gut feeling was being

proven.

"Because all the evidence points to the bones being buried in the 1880s."

Carol studied Roger's face as he considered her words. She continued, "I believe Harry realized these graves existed and saw ghosts when he was a young boy. Charlie confirms the ghosts are real, but he's concerned they may not want his help."

Roger chuckled, "The ghosts are real and real upset." He put his hand on Carol's and in a hushed voice said, "Don't tell Harry yet. I need to help him in a few areas other than the ghosts." Turning serious, he added, "This can't go beyond us. Harry suffered abuse when he was nine years old, and his father may have been involved. Because of the trauma, he either formed an alternate personality or had a complete breakdown and became fixated on his dreams and the ghosts. It's going to take time for me to guide him toward a better mental place."

"Can I help?" Carol grasped Roger's hand. "You know I like Harry, a lot. Let me know what I can do to help."

"I'm sure you can and will help. My work with Harry will depend on how long it takes to dig up the rest of the graves?"

Carol's eyes became distant as she considered his question. "The boys have finished three graves this morning. That leaves nine more to examine. I don't expect any surprises in the graves. The surprises will come as we try to understand how this happened to Harry and why these spirits remained together as a group, in his backyard."

Carol stood and walked around the patio. "I'm fearing for our well-being here. Last night those ghosts physically hurt Charlie. That's not a normal situation, and even if we're careful, we can't control what they will do."

"I agree. Do you have any suggestions?" Roger stood and walked toward her. "Perhaps we should meet with Charlie and get his advice. It looks like he will be the one dealing with the dead." Roger laughed. "Shit. It sounds like we have a *Walking Dead Episode* ahead of us, doesn't it?"

Carol turned and smiled. "Roger, don't be silly. They are ghosts, not zombies."

"Yes, but they are dead, and they are walking around the yard, or they were. Harry thinks they're staying away to avoid Charlie. He feels they know Charlie can see them. That makes the ghosts even more dangerous, because it indicates intelligence, awareness, and intent."

Harry walked up to the two and cleared his throat. "Is it a pow-wow? The two of you look way too intent to be talking about the weather. So, what's up? Am I guilty?"

Roger stumbled on his words, and it came out as, "Ah... Well... Look, Harry. We were talking about you, and I was going to hold off telling you what Carol's team found. But you will know eventually. They dated the bones to the 1880s. There is no way you could have buried or killed these people, Harry."

Harry noticed Caseville Man, Farmer Bill, and the last man he buried, Arnold, standing at the edge of the woods. *Odd,* he thought. *Arnold hardly ever shows up. I wonder why he's here?*

They began approaching. Soon sixteen ghosts stood behind Carol and Roger. "The ghosts are here. All of them. Standing behind you."

The two looked around. Roger turned to Harry. "I don't see them, but I feel a presence... overly calm and a chill in the air."

Carol agreed. "Same here. What are they doing?"

Before Harry could say, Charlie touched his back. Harry jumped. "What the hell," he turned and saw Charlie. "Do you see them?"

Charlie laughed, "Yes, of course... I see Roger and Carol. Who else is here? The ghosts?"

"Yes, the ghosts," insisted Harry.

Charlie smiled. "Nope, none here. Come on, Harry, let's take a walk." He pulled Harry toward the mobile home. When they were ten feet from the patio, he whispered. "I did see them, Harry. If I ignore them, they might believe I can't see them and ignore me. I've never experienced ghosts like these... it's as if they are still alive, looking the same as the day they died."

Harry agreed. "When we go back, don't talk about them. Let's see what they do."

The two men walked back to a bewildered Roger and Carol. Roger said, "What's going on with you two?"

Harry and Charlie spoke simultaneously, "We... I.... No, you go... Sorry..."

Harry indicated for Charlie to speak. "Go ahead."

"I was asking Harry if we could go into town for lunch."

The others checked the time, and indeed, it was almost one o'clock. The morning was gone and lunch was missed.

"Great idea, isn't it?" asked Harry.

Carol nodded. "What about the ghosts you were so concerned about a minute ago?"

Harry answered, "They're not going anywhere, Carol. Why don't we all freshen up and drive into town? There's a nice steakhouse in Bad Axe where we can have a meal, drink, and talk openly." Caseville Man, Farmer Bill, and Arnold watched Harry speak. They turned away and drifted toward the back of the yard and into the woods.

Charlie exhaled and said, "As the kids say in Ann Arbor, they're gone." The sound of the backhoe stopped and Jonathon approached the team. "What's going on here? I hope it has to do with lunch and not ghosts."

"Yes, we're going to Bad Axe." Carol said. "Could you please let Lila know? She was working on Clarence... Harry calls him the Caseville Man."

CHAPTER 21

Carol whispered to Harry, "We can talk in your car. I'll make sure the kids ride with Roger. You don't mind, do you?"

"Good idea. Tell them I want to show you the area and tell them to order our meals. I'll have the soup and salad special. We can arrive at the restaurant before the food arrives. Is that enough quiet time for you?"

She laughed and put her arm around him. "Yes, that's plenty of time, for now."

"Grandma," Charlie yelled as he approached. "Sorry, *Carol*... I'm riding with you into town. Those two idiots are driving me crazy, and you don't want me to go crazy, do you?"

"If that's what it takes, then yes... go crazy, because you are riding with them. I have to talk to Harry in private, so we're going to be about twenty minutes late to lunch. Order the soup and salad special for both of us."

Charlie was obviously disappointed, but he kept his cool and only whimpered a little "Shit," and walked away.

Carol ran into the house, passed Roger in the hallway, side-swiped Harry, and ran up the stairs. She yelled down, "I'll need the bathroom," but no one heard her.

In the motorhome, Charlie was first in the bathroom.

"You little twerp," yelled Lila. "Don't you know it's always ladies first?"

"That's only if you're a lady... you're not." Charlie yelled back.

On Lila's way from her bedroom, she passed the bathroom door and said, "Hand me my bag."

A grinning Charlie handed her the toiletry bag. "Here you

go, *sweetheart*. I'm done, so if you hurry you can get in here before Iron Man." Feeling refreshed, he walked through the motorhome and noticed Jonathon sitting quietly on the couch, untying his shoes.

"She's in the bathroom, right?" Jonathon looked up and asked. "I think you two have a system in place to deny me access to that room. So I used the kitchen sink to clean up."

"Is that what they taught you in the Army?"

"Yes, be resourceful." Jonathon said as he stood. "Did you finish the last grave?"

"No, you finished after they announced lunch break. I did everything else, and we have ghosts. I watched them, but they didn't mess with me, again."

Lila walked out of the bathroom and grabbed her things. "Let's go boys; we don't want to be late."

"Ladies first," Charlie said as he opened the door for Jonathon.

"Hilarious, kid; keep it up and you'll be in worse shape than you were last night," Jonathon retorted.

Charlie laughed and ran behind him, leaving Lila to shut and lock the mobile home. She was used to being the brunt of the men's jokes. She grew up with four brothers and was stronger than any of them. Not physically, but mentally.

Roger insisted Lila would ride shotgun, even though Charlie called it first. After some grumbling, they were on the road for the short drive to Bad Axe.

Harry and Carol drove in the opposite direction. Carol talked while Harry drove.

"Did you here Roger say the graves are older than you are?" Carol watched Harry's hardened face, studied his short beard, and admired his full head of salt and pepper hair.

"Yes. If my reasoning is correct, I am off the hook for the crimes I have imagined all these years. It will take time to understand what happened, but I'm sure Roger has a theory." Harry turned down a gravel road and stopped the car on the shoulder.

Statuesque white windmills dotted the landscape. Carol placed her hand on Harry's thigh. "Roger said they abused you when you were nine. I'm not supposed to say anything until he talks to you, but to hell with Roger."

Harry smiled. "I find it hard to believe that I have been carrying this burden my entire life, and now it's supposed to be over? What about the ghosts?"

"My team will deal with them. It's not our first time. With your help, Charlie's help, and the help of a girl I know in Detroit, I think we can get these poor souls on their way home."

"And me. Where do I fit in?" Harry squeezed her hand and smiled.

"You fit right in with my plans, and hopefully I fit into yours."

"I guess they do. Thank God you're into ghosts... can you see them, too?"

"Yes, a few times in the past. Charlie is the sensitive one. I formed this team because of him. Two years ago, I was working on a case involving a young girl. Charlie was helping me in the lab and saw the young girl's ghost in the room. Through him, I could put together a composite of the girl's killer. We solved the case and Charlie helped the ghost move on."

A warm feeling of joy filled Harry's heart as the weight of a lifetime of fear and remorse released its grip on him. He could feel the pressure releasing as tears of joy ran down his cheeks.

The expression on Carol's face answered his questions.

"Wow," he responded to the love he saw within her and the powerful aura surrounding her. "We better get lunch. It looks like we have a lot of work to do and fun to begin."

Carol stretched around the center console of Harry's SUV

and positioned herself across his body. She kissed him... her hand noticed he was as excited as she was.

"Yes, we have a future." she smiled and kissed him again. "I don't want you to stop; we can't miss our lunch meeting. I hope we can continue this moment tonight, after dinner."

Harry said little as he drove to Bad Axe. Carol was busy checking her notebook and phone. *Is this what I want?* he asked himself. *It seems too much like a repeat of Kathy.*

"Harry, are you OK?"

"Yes, I'm fine. Still dizzy from the idea that I might not be a crazy killer, and a little gun shy about our budding relationship. There's been so many secrets and lies that I have lived through that I don't know if I'm up to more."

"You have a valid point. I will try to be as honest as I can. The reason I want to be in your life is because of the relationship I had with your wife. She talked about you whenever I was with her."

Harry burst out laughing. "So, I'm your knight in shining armor. Carol, I like you. You made me laugh again... it helped. I want to be a member of your team, but we will take it slow on our relationship. And that's a deal buster."

"Yes, Sir." She smiled to herself and relaxed.

CHAPTER 22

As the team inhaled their lunch, Carol worked on her notebook. Charlie selected a secluded table for six. "Good job, Charlie." she whispered.

After the server cleared the table and refreshed their drinks, Carol leaned into the table and spoke. "We have ghosts. Charlie and Harry can see them. Our team is growing and I love and welcome you all. When we get back to Harry's, our very own *Iron Man* will continue his earth moving abilities. Roger, I want you and Harry to dig into the history of the property. There must be a record of this graveyard, and I want to resolve this case before the end of the month. That gives us less than two weeks."

"Carol," Roger said, "When will Tianna be here?"

Charlie's ears perked up. His phone went blank, and he removed the earpiece. "Well, Carol... when will she be here?"

"Tomorrow, mid-morning. Beware..." In her voice of authority, "If she doesn't like us, she's going back home tomorrow. She has to like and respect us, so be good. No funny business... boys, and girl. Am I making myself understood?"

"Yes, Carol... Yes, Grandma.... Yes, Dear... Yes, Madam... If I have to, Carol."

Charlie was suddenly engaged in the conversation. "I'll be good, Carol."

"I know," Carol lied. She understands her grandson because he's a lot like her. The problem? She understands him too well, contributing to her lack of complete trust.

Jonathon and Lila argued all the way back to the graveyard. Charlie's eyes were glued to his phone, and Roger asked himself, *when did I lose control of my case?* Then he remembered, *Oh, yes. Carol talked me into joining her team. I need to talk about a contract, story rights...*

"Roger," Jonathon said, "You can shut the car off."

Roger turned the ignition and pulled the key. "I was thinking about this case. It appears Carol likes to be in total control?"

"Yes, so does her Wonder Woman, Lila Budd. They make a great pair. I keep wondering what they do in that trailer. And Charlie is some kind of freak... if you ask me."

"Jonathon, you said your drinks were ice tea. I think you're buzzed."

"Yes, Sir. Buzzed."

"Can I ask you a question?"

"Yes, Sir?"

"Why are you here? I can understand Lila and grandson Charlie. Even Harry brings the ghosts and the ability to see them. What do you bring to this team?"

"Sir, I am Iron Man. I do the fucking hard work... electronics, IT, computer programming, and research. Today it's excavation. I kind of like being a blue-collar worker. Oh, and I am sort of the FBI agent."

"What does... *sort of...* mean?"

"I freelance... The FBI knows we're here and what we do. They gave me a badge and we work cases like this, giving them total deniability."

"Amazing. See what a little sharing can do?"

"You better not have hypnotized me. I know how to kill."

"So do I. You better get to work or those two women will be angry." They both watched Carol and Lila approach.

"Let's get to work, boys." She gave Roger a quick hug. "We can talk before dinner. Harry says he's making Italian for us all."

"Yes. That will be nice. I better start my search for information on this property."

Roger reached Harry's back door and turned. The mounds of dirt, Jonathon now digging, Charlie holding a shovel, watching. *How should I handle Harry?*

"Roger. Are you coming in?" Harry said through the screen door.

"Yes, we need to talk, but first I want a hug." Harry opened his arms and the two men hugged.

Harry pulled back. "Roger, you were correct in your observations. I understand I am not the killer, as you predicted."

"I knew you weren't a killer from the moment I spoke to you."

"Sure, and I'm a teenager." Harry questioned why he used *teenager. Perhaps because I feel like the teenager I never was. 'Don't pity yourself, old man,'* he told himself.

Roger chuckled and walked into the kitchen. "Are you OK?"

"Everyone keeps asking me that. Yes. I am OK. It's going to take work, but I will learn to like myself and accept the past."

"We must keep our sessions going once a day, at least until the team is done with the investigation; then once a month."

"That's fine. How long are you staying here?" Harry felt caged.

"I leave with the team... perhaps a week or two. Carol said you would drive down to Ann Arbor to help the team as needed."

"Yes, and she will be a regular visitor in my Port Austin home. We're working on a relationship."

"Good," Roger said, "slow is always good when dealing with Caroline. She can overpower, can't she?"

Harry laughed. "You know her well?"

"Yes. I have known her for many years. We tried dating, but I was a little too *gay* for her. Go figure."

Harry burst out laughing. "Are you kidding? She slept with my wife, but you're too gay?"

"She did?" Roger didn't wait for the answer. "I wonder if that's why she's fascinated by you, besides your ability to see ghosts. It is a challenge trying to figure out what is in Carol's head. She is not a typical woman."

"True. I think that fascinates me. Carol is so much like my Kathy, and I loved her even more than you can imagine."

Roger stepped into his doctor role and said, "Harry, don't make the same mistake. You married Kathy because she was safe, but you are not the same man you were. You do not have to run away from your past, so take time to find the real you. There are still ghosts in the graveyard outside, and inside... deep in your subconscious. Until you come to grips with all of them, you will not be free from their influence."

CHAPTER 23

The battle raged on between Jonathon and Charlie. It irked Jonathon that Charlie was smart and a smart-ass at the same time. And for Charlie, Jonathon was like an older brother he could irritate.

Charlie watched Jonathon scooping bucket loads of dirt from grave number eight. He looked at his copy of the list of victims and read... *(Orville) A big man in his mid-fifties with only one leg.* Having seen several of the ghosts, he wondered which one assaulted him first. *I would love to get even with that one. Perhaps throw away a leg bone or two?* He laughed at the idea. Unfortunately, *Carol would become angry, and that could be suicide.*

Jonathon stopped and jumped off the backhoe. Standing behind it, he undid his jeans and relieved himself. Charlie yelled, "It's not nice to piss on the ghosts. They'll get even with you tonight, so if you wake up all wet you'll know what happened."

"Hilarious. Don't you have something to do, other than watch me piss?"

"I'm caught up. I wish Carol and Lila would let me uncover and gather the bones, instead of just preparing them," Charlie said.

"You're not a forensic expert, and it's too important to trust a beginner. Charlie, you're more like me than you thought. Just another bull in the pasture, following the stupid cows around."

Charlie laughed. "I'm telling Grandma and Lila that you

called them stupid cows. That should put you in the doghouse. No sex for you tonight, John Boy."

"Fuck off, twerp. You're such a little asshole. I don't know why I even try to be nice to you." Jonathon flashed a finger at Charlie as he climbed onto the backhoe. "If you were a real *man*, you would volunteer to run this damn machine and share the workload. But no, you just complain about the job you've got."

"I wouldn't mind helping you, but you're doing such an outstanding job. Better than I could ever do. I'll see if they want me to help with..." he checked Harry's list, and added, "Jimmy. That's number seven... the one I just finished. It says here, he was a young man with a crushed skull. I wonder how that happened?"

Jonathon couldn't hear him over the backhoe engine. Charlie looked toward the woods and saw the ghost of the young man with his head crushed on one side. *Don't look at him,* he told himself, and turned. *For a teenager, he appeared older and hardened. I bet he got his head crushed by some old fart like Jonathon.*

Charlie smirked, turned toward the woods, and observed that Jimmy wasn't alone now. Two younger women, one a teenager, were holding hands. *That's odd. They almost look like a couple.* Jimmy grabbed the youngest girl's shoulder and, in a whisper, spoke to her. She pulled her hand from the older girl and took Jimmy's hand. The group returned to the woods and dissolved into a mist.

Harry placed his hand on Charlie's shoulder.

"What the hell?" Charlie said... startled and nervous.

"You saw them, didn't you?"

"Yes, who are the girls? The one looks like she's my age."

Harry smiled. "Cora was seventeen when I... when someone put her in the grave."

"It's going to take time, Sir. It's got to be difficult learning that your life was a bad dream." Charlie smiled. "How did Cora die?"

Harry thought. "She had a bullet in her skull and was black and blue. A terrible fight might have caused her death. The night she died, a young man also died. Robert. Yes, his name was Robert, and he also had a bullet hole in his head."

"You care about these people, don't you?"

Tears filled Harry's eyes. "Yes, very much so." He collected himself, wiped his eyes, and added, "Roger and I are driving into town. Will you tell Carol?"

"Sure, what's up?"

"We hope to find some information about this property. Hopefully the County Register of Deeds office will have the original paperwork." From the corner of his eye, he saw Cora and Anna return. They were holding hands and walking around Anna's grave.

Jonathon moved the backhoe to the young woman's grave, turned the engine off, and walked toward Harry and Charlie. "I'll be starting Anna's grave now. Charlie you can finish hand-digging Orville's grave when you're done here." He turned to Harry and put his arm over the older man's shoulder. "I hope you're coping with all this, but then I think you're quite a powerful man. Most people would have ended up in the psych ward of some lonely hospital." He pulled his hand away and smiled. "What's Roger up to?"

Harry saw Jonathon's eyes looking toward the garage. Roger put his notepad into the back seat, shut the door, and walked toward the three men.

"We are driving into town for research. I'm not sure..." Before he could finish, he heard Carol calling.

"Charlie, is Jimmy ready for me?"

"Yes, Carol. I was on my way to tell you."

Carol picked up a plastic container and walked toward the

men. "Is this a men's only gathering?"

"No," Charlie retorted. "There are two girls standing over there looking at Anna's grave. When everyone turned toward the white grave marker, the two girls dissolved into a mist.

"Gone. That was quick," chuckled Harry.

Roger took Carol aside and told her where he was going. "Do you want us to bring back dinner, or are you guys working late tonight?"

"We're on schedule... what time will you be back?"

Roger mulled the question and asked, "When do you want us to be back?"

"We'll finish here by five and be cleaned up for dinner by six. How is Harry doing, have you learned more about his childhood, and did he tell you what we talked about before lunch?"

"OK... No... Yes."

"I take it you're angry with me. I came on to Harry because I want us to have a relationship but, I needed him to tell me to go slow. Now he is aware I'm interested, but he can control how quickly it proceeds. It's now under his control."

"You have never been under any man's control, Carol."

"Roger," Harry interrupted. "Let's get going." He smiled at Carol and guided Roger toward the car. He looked back at the team and added, "We'll be back with Chinese take-out, so work up an appetite."

CHAPTER 24

Being a short drive, neither of the men had much to say. Roger played with his notebook while a million thoughts ran through Harry's mind as he drove. The local radio station, WLEW, announced, "Sheriff McNabb reported this morning that he is not aware of any investigation by the FBI in his jurisdiction. *There should be no reason for alarm. Trust me, the rumors are all false,* were his exact words."

Both Roger and Harry's ears perked up. They looked at each other, and Harry said, "Oh shit. We have to talk to the sheriff and explain what the hell's going on."

Roger nodded. "Let me talk. We can have him come to the site and make him a part of what's happening. If he learns about the ghosts, all the better. That way he'll never tell, for fear of being laughed at behind his back and at the voting booth."

Harry laughed. "Roger, you think like a con man I know in Grand Rapids. He's very high in state politics. Have McNabb come over when we're meeting the girl from Detroit. That way we can clue the team about our devious plan of action."

The car pulled up to the Huron County sheriff's office. Harry took his phone from his vest pocket and flipped through the contacts. After a few minutes, he was talking. "Jim, Harry here in Bad Axe. I need a favor...

"Yes, thank you, but I am doing well... might even be back in the dating game again. But..."

Harry was talking to a high-ranking FBI agent he represented. The verdict was a large settlement. The agent agreed to fax the sheriff for confirmation that the Ann Arbor forensics expert in Bad Axe is in charge of the investigation and the FBI demands full cooperation.

Sheriff McNabb was standing at the fax machine holding a paper. He turned to the two men and said, "Well, I guess I need to call another press conference."

"Hell, all you need to do is call three people and have the radio record your statement."

"I don't understand," the sheriff said, as he led the two men into his office. "Coffee? Marge, get three mugs of coffee in here, please. So Harry, I thought you were going insane and out of your mind."

Roger started, "Sir, that's my fault…"

"Roger, stop." He turned to the sheriff and said, "I discovered a grave with sixteen caskets from the 1880s on my property." Harry watched for a reaction… none. "Roger helped me deal with the ghosts from my past and reported the find. There is no crime, just a bunch of bones that need to be moved."

Roger listened to the story and nodded. "We have an issue. Ghosts might have attached themselves to the bones."

McNabb burst out laughing. The big man looked like he was going to explode. "You got me there, Doctor. That's a good one, but I don't think it will make it into the news release. So when are you going to be out of my county? I'm afraid there might be gawkers arriving soon if I don't do something."

Harry mulled the problem and replied, "Can you block off the road from my property to the end of the mile. There aren't any other homes between them."

McNabb looked pleased. "I'll get the road crew to set up the blockade this afternoon. Just drive around them if they are up when you head back home."

Roger stood. "Sheriff, would you come to the excavation site tomorrow morning around nine, and plan on being there for a few hours. Perhaps until lunch. We need you to be involved. Your expertise is welcome."

McNabb's face was beaming. "I'll try. Now, you boys get back there and see that those poor souls find their new home. You know we like to take care of our own."

Harry and Roger later commented on how prophetic the sheriff's words were. Roger commented, "I guess that sums up what we have to do, doesn't it?"

The register of deeds was in the same building, so Harry led the way to the elevator and then the office. The office staff was eager to help. They made copies of the papers they could find and listed the ones missing or lost in the fire of 1871. Roger paid for the copies, and as they walked to the elevator, he suggested, "Let's go to the bar across the street. I think it's called Pete's."

"And how do you know about Pete's bar?" Harry asked.

"I saw it through the window and I got thirsty thinking about a scotch and water."

"What are you, an alcoholic psychiatrist?"

"Not yet, I don't think... I mean... I don't drink in the morning."

"You did the other day, and you talked me into drinking too."

Roger opened the door and followed Harry into the bright sunlight. There wasn't a cloud in the sky, and the little town was almost surreal as the two walked into the historic village tavern. Eyes turned toward them... someone yelled, "Harry, you old bastard. How's it going? I hear your house on the lake is getting a makeover?"

The shadow of a tall, slender man approached Harry. As the light of the window cast on the man's face, he realized it was his boyhood friend, Tommy. Roger watched as the two men hugged, pulled apart, and laughed. "Where have you been?" Harry asked first.

"I was in the Army, stationed in Japan, and I stayed there until a few years ago." His eyes burned into Harry's. "I kept tabs on you, on the news and the local gossip. I understand there's something going on in your neighborhood?"

Harry wasn't sure what to do or say. Seeing Tommy after all these years was unexpected.

Roger sensed the situation and approached Tommy. "I'm Harry's friend and doctor. We're here for a drink. If you want to join us, you're welcome." He touched Tommy's arm, smiled, and ran his hand down to Tommy's hand. "I'm Dr. Roger Jahosibad. You're Tommy. Now, don't tell me you're the Tommy from Harry's teen years? He's told me stories about the two of you."

The bartender approached the three men. "Tommy, are you getting your friends a drink?"

"Yes, sure Jerry. So, anything the two of you want... it's on me."

The three sat down. Harry composed himself and spoke. "Tommy, we found a grave on my property. That's what the rumors are about, and yes my lakeshore home is being remodeled. The builder kicked me out because they had to remove a lot of nasty stuff. I think he mentioned asbestos. I'm staying at the homestead. Tommy, I just can't picture you in the Army. Amazing. What are you doing these days?"

"Retired. But hey, I have to go." He chugged his beer and excused himself. On the way out he whispered to a group of men in the back of the barroom and left through the back door.

Roger laughed. "Looks like Tommy has problems too. Perhaps he saw a ghost or two?"

"I guess. He was my best friend, but times change and so do people. Look at me, a successful lawyer, well off, and healthy. Who would guess I have ghosts in my backyard?"

"Not me, that's for sure."

CHAPTER 25

Harry spoke to the bartender as he paid the tab and acquired the directions to the library. He knew where it was, but the question smoothed the conversation he wanted to have about Tommy. Harry explained how he knew Tommy and how he lost touch during high school and after.

The bartender mentioned Tommy suffered during his tour in Vietnam and he now has post-traumatic stress disorder.

"That's a shame," said Harry. "Well, thank you Bob. I'll be back again soon."

Harry suggested walking to the library, but Roger insisted on moving the car away from the front of the bar. "You don't want some of Tommy's buddies taking perceived revenge against you," he advised.

Harry wasn't sure why Tommy would want revenge, but he agreed. "The library is around the corner, but we'll have to drive a few blocks to get there."

Once the car was in the library's parking lot, Harry asked, "Why do you think Tommy's buddies would seek revenge?"

"I saw how they were looking at you. It appears Tommy has been talking about you negatively. You realize he has a mental illness, don't you?"

"Yes, he has post-traumatic stress disorder." Harry knew several men who came back from Vietnam and the Middle East with mental problems, but he never thought much about it, other than knowing it was a thing. "Can't he get treatment?"

"Yes, but he has to seek it. I have helped many people using cognitive-behavioral therapy (CBT). The idea is to change the thought patterns that are disturbing his life. Tommy is functional. He said he stayed in the military after Nam, so he can't be too bad. Perhaps without the discipline of the Army, and being an alcoholic, he is now facing all of his demons, like you are."

"Like me?" Harry questioned.

"Yes, like you. We can talk about him later." Roger stepped out of the car and waited for Harry. "I'll find the books, while you talk to the librarian. I'm sure they have an old plat map of the farms and homes, and if we're lucky, they'll have one from the 1880s."

Harry was thinking about Tommy and didn't respond. He walked into the library and approached the woman behind the counter, while Roger walked around looking for the history section.

The portly young woman sitting at the counter smiled and asked, "Can I help you with something, Sir?"

"Yes, I need information about the family home I grew up in, south of here. My name is Harold Essen, and my parents bought the home from a farmer, and I am searching for its history."

"Have you tried the County Registrar's office? They would have the deeds for that land," she said with a pleasant smile.

"Yes, we just came from there. Some records are incomplete because of the fires in the 1880s. All we can find is the farmer who Dad purchased the home from and Dad and Mom's deed. I think the house was part of a larger farm, and they sold the land and home as one. Then the farmer created a new deed for just the home. It gets a little complicated, but we need to know what happened there. See, we found a graveyard that was never recorded."

The moment Harry told her about the graveyard, he knew it was a mistake. Her face lit up like a headlight on a dark night. She said, "Oh my, a graveyard. Do you know who is buried there?"

"Dead people." Harry smiled, hoping to change the tone of the conversation.

"Very funny, Sir." She stood and directed Harry to where Roger was intently reading a plat map. "It seems your friend has found the book I was going to suggest. There are two of them, one from 1890 and another from 1904. If you would like, we have digital versions of the books that you could download and take with you."

The woman pulled a tattered book from a display on Bad Axe history. "This is an early history of Bad Axe. I'm not sure if it will have anything you are looking for, but it will cover the major events, including the fires that destroyed Bad Axe in the 1880s, a tragedy of enormous magnitude."

Harry thanked her and thought about the tragedy that his ghosts cost him. A lifetime of living with demons that were not of his making. The loss he felt, he couldn't explain or comprehend. Thoughts of what could have been crept into his mind.

No. I can't go there. he insisted. *What was... was. I am the man, I am because of what I suffered throughout my life. I have no reason to resent or complain. It is what it is.* Still, there was an overall sadness that filled his heart. A tremendous loss.

***

Roger and Harry studied while talking about the history they were finding. The two men, having shared Harry's life story, were becoming friends, as well as a doctor and patient. They formed a bond that they both appreciated.

"You know, Harry, I'm glad you didn't kill those sixteen people. I'm not sure how I would feel about you." Roger laughed. "Perhaps I would have found that attractive. Not that I would suggest..."

"Shut up, Roger," Harry replied. "Just because you're gay,

doesn't give you a special license to suggest that I should be. I am not homophobic, but I like my friends to respect that I am attracted to them only as male friends. You are a friend."

"Understood, Harry," Roger said. "Are we ready to order takeout from the Chinese restaurant?"

"Yes, It's *China King*. Why don't you walk across the road, past the sheriff's office and use the restaurant's back door? Here is the list Carol gave me. I marked my choice too. You can pay for it."

"Sure, make the gay guy pay."

Harry broke out laughing and the librarian moved closer to them, sending warning looks his way. "You should pay the bill; they're your team."

Roger gathered his notepad and papers. "Here are two pages I would like copies of. I used my notepad to make photographs, but I see they make copies for a fee." He handed the book to Harry and added, "I'll call when the order is ready, so you can pick me up."

Harry wasn't listening, but nodded in agreement. He was reading a list of the churches in Bad Axe during the 1880s. *Nothing*, he thought. *An unknown grave behind a building... must have meant that it was a church. But there's nothing listed. Not before or after. I know my victims.* He looked up at the librarian. *Stop it*, he thought. *You didn't kill them. But I know them and they are not one big, happy, dead family.*

CHAPTER 26

Harry and Roger pulled into the driveway at five-thirty. There was no sign of the team, but Roger noted that there were only three graves to finish digging.

Roger stepped out and opened the back door. "They must all be getting ready to eat. I guess we timed it well."

Harry helped Roger with the bags of food and when they reached the back door, it opened.

"Carol," Roger said. "Thank you." He worked his way in, passing the open door to Harry.

"Why so many bags?" Carol asked.

"Big servings," responded Harry.

Carol laughed. "So, now the two of you are talking *for* each other? What the hell happened in that little town? You leave here as two normal men, well sort of normal, and come back buddies?"

Roger put his bags on the counter as Harry piled his on the table where Lila and Jonathon were sitting.

Lila spoke up, "Carol, don't pick on them. Maybe Roger, here, turned Harry gay."

Jonathon burst out laughing. "Lilly, babe, watch your mouth... these are two respected men you're talking about. I mean, Roger is smooth, a little old, but still a kid next to Harry over there, and that would be a strange arrangement." He pulled Lila back into her chair and continued, "On second thought, Carol, pick on them. But remember, they pay the bills."

Harry ignored the comments, for the moment, and began

setting the table for dinner while Carol and Roger talked in the doorway. Charlie pulled the door open from the outside, causing Roger to fall through the door. The teen was quick enough to catch him and apologize for the accident.

Carol chastised her grandson. "Charlie, you need to be careful. I keep telling you, *slow down and take your time.*"

"Grandma, I said I was sorry. When is dinner?" he asked, walking along the counter, looking at the piles of Chinese food.

Harry announced in a firm voice, "There is wine in the cooler, and tonight everyone will have some wine." He winked at Charlie. "This is my treat... well... Roger paid for it, but he's doing it for me. You are all doing this for me. Thank you, and let's eat."

Carol put an arm around Harry and said, "Charlie, get a glass of wine for me while you get yours." She squeezed Harry and patted his backside, whispering, "I like the way you're taking more command. This is how I see you on our team."

"Is that what you told Roger, too?" Harry chuckled and winked at her. "The moo-goo-guy porky thing looks good." He placed a spoonful on his plate, next to sweet and sour chicken and rice, added an egg roll and green beans.

Carol followed him outdoors to the patio. Roger and Charlie filled their plates and sat at the kitchen table with Lila and Jonathon. None of them spoke, but sounds of food being inhaled filled the air. Harry rushed back in and poured himself a glass of wine. He walked back, carrying a full bottle with him.

Charlie was first to the finish line; he put his paper plate in the basket and walked outside. Soon Lila and Jonathon had the kitchen put back together. Jonathon put his arm around her small waist and pulled her closer. His hand traced her spine as he spoke. "Are you ready for dessert?"

"Not yet. I want to hear what Roger and Harry learned. I'll

tell you when I'm ready." She stretched, licked his lower lip, and said. "Ooh, tasty."

"You're sick, Lila, and I love it."

Carol and Harry sat at the end of the patio table with their backs to the graveyard. Charlie sat across the table facing them, Lila alongside Roger, and Jonathon stood behind them, his arms folded and feet apart. As Charlie would say, *military style*.

Harry thought about standing, decided not to, then remembered his years as a court lawyer. *Why not?* he thought. *Indeed, why not?* He cleared his throat. "I can relate to those in prison who prove they were not guilty, and can go home. Have fun putting your life back together, my friend."

He looked at Charlie and smiled. "I don't envy the young. I had a loss that took my youth and turned it into a living hell. Roger and I are still working on that one, but I am understanding and see that I have a future. I'm not sure I can see ghosts other than those standing behind me, though."

Charlie smiled, Lila squeezed Jonathon's hand, Roger made a note in his notepad, and Harry turned to Carol. "If you think I can be of help to your team, I will join you, provided we can get my ghosts to pass on. Is there really a bright light they need to walk through?"

"Yes, there is," responded Carol.

"Yes," added Charlie.

Harry sat, poured a glass of wine, and said, "Your show, Carol."

Carol didn't stand, but leaned forward with her hands apart on the table. "I talked to Roger and Harry about the information they unearthed in Bad Axe. History is always the first place we look *toward,* to solve the problems of today. We found that the history of the bones cleared Harry of any crime. Tianna will be here in the morning, and, with her help, we will delve into the spirit world and learn the history of these people."

"Grandma, you said I could work with her. Please don't go back on your word, again."

"Charlie, it's Carol, and if Tianna approves, you can work with her. It will be an excellent education for you both."

Charlie formed a thumbs up with his hand and walked toward Jonathon. He whispered, "There might be some trouble before morning. The ghosts are all standing in a circle, and it appears there is a fire in the middle."

"Fire? Can I look or will they see me and rape me, too? Like they did you?" He chuckled at the thought.

"Fuck you. I'm trying to be serious here, and yes... look and tell me if there is a fire in the woods."

Jonathon turned, looked, and then walked into the garage. He returned with two beers and handed one to Charlie. "No fire, no ghosts, nada. Are you sure you don't take drugs?"

"No drugs, John Boy. Just brains and perception. Something you lost in the military, I would imagine. Thanks for the beer."

"No problem, kid. If those ghosts start something, what should I do, being I can't see them?

"Run and don't bend down." Charlie chuckled and walked back into the kitchen. Someone stacked the leftovers in the refrigerator. He reached in and pulled out an egg roll, dipped it into some sweet and sour sauce, and took his beer into the backyard. The ghosts stood at the edge of the woods. But as long as he ignored them, they didn't become alarmed.

Sitting on the grass with his legs crossed, he took his phone out, set up his earbuds, and called his friend, Elizabeth, from Ann Arbor.

"Hi, Liz... Yes, it's Charlie and I'm fine. I'm in Bad Axe with Grandma and her team. We're talking to ghosts, or at least we hope to. I just need to talk to someone sane, and you're the sanest person I know. ... Stop laughing, Liz. You are too sane.

Charlie listened for several minutes while Elizabeth caught

him up on the latest at school. She was an eagle at heart. Brave and able to see things better than most girls, while Charlie lived within his mind... in the moment.

"Liz, the girl I told you about, Tianna, from Detroit. I'm meeting her in the morning. Anything I need to remember?"

Elizabeth laughed. "Charlie, you're such a little boy. Just remember that girls are human too. Be kind, polite, and don't show off. Let it happen, and soon you might have a new friend who is a girl."

"You make it sound so easy. Every time I try to relax around a sexy girl my age, I go into convulsions and run away, into my mind. Somehow I'm getting a vibe from Tianna and we've never met."

"You and your psychic vibes and feelings. Is she a ghost nut, like you? If so, Charlie, you're in for a treat, unless she has a boyfriend. Well?"

"I don't know. Shit, something else to worry about tonight. Thanks. That helped a bunch. She's so hot, Liz. Grandma showed me some videos and photographs. She's Black and American Indian. Hot, long, black hair, smoky black eyes, thin but not skinny."

Charlie heard his name called and looked to see his grandmother looking toward him. He checked the ghosts. They were still in their circle. "Liz, Grandma wants me. Love you, and I'll call tomorrow night to let you know if I scored."

"Don't you dare try to score. Just communicate and learn."

"OK... To me that's the same thing." He stood and waved at Carol. "I'm coming, Carol." He yelled and checked himself. There was a wetness, adjusted his pants, and pulled his shirt down. "I'm coming," he repeated, and walked toward the patio table.

CHAPTER 27

Charlie couldn't concentrate. Tianna became an obsession, and he tried to understand his feelings, but couldn't. *I feel like I'm going to meet my soulmate... Odd. Too odd,* He thought, *I haven't even met her, yet. What if she doesn't like me? What if she hates me? Why do I want her so badly? Is there a spiritual connection? Are the ghosts putting these feelings into my mind? Why?*

He walked toward the three ghosts at the edge of the woods. "Hey, you fuckers. Are you driving me crazy, like Harry?"

Lila heard him yelling at the trees. "Charlie, why don't you go into the motorhome and take care of yourself. You're a mess." She grew closer and saw his face. "Can I help?"

Charlie half smiled. "I'm worked up about Tianna's arrival in the morning. I have this thing, a feeling as much as anything, and questions. I sense that we'll be close, very close. Sort of like kindred spirits."

Lila laughed, "So now you're a psychic, too? But, why were you yelling at the trees?"

"Perhaps I am psychic." He looked toward the ghosts and added, "I wasn't yelling at the trees." He raised his hand and pointed. "There are three ghosts standing there, watching us. I yelled at them because I hope they aren't doing to me what they did to Harry."

"That's fucking crazy. Have you talked to Roger about these feelings?"

"No. Should I?"

"I don't know. It sounds like you're getting involved deeper than you want to be. You're always so calm with the ghosts." She watched the woods, hoping perhaps to grab a glimpse.

Lila never saw a ghost. The team had ten legitimate ghost sightings in the past year. Charlie always sees them, Carol sees a few, but Lila? *Never. Not once,* she thought. *Is there something wrong with me? I can see their images on film, and hear their recorded voices, well... sometimes.*

Charlie put his hand over Lila's shoulder. "Let's leave the ghosts for Tianna. At least tonight they aren't picking on me... yet."

Lila laughed, "See, I made everything OK. You're better, I'm good, and I hope Jonathon is ready for bed."

"Damn, Lila. Do you ever take a breather from sex?"

"Not if I can help it."

The two laughed and walked into the motorhome. Charlie headed straight for the bathroom. "I might be awhile."

Jonathon and Lila interrupted their kiss to say. "OK."

***

Roger and Carol poured over the historical records, while Harry read a detective novel. He wasn't reading; he was thinking about the last fifty-six years of his life. *A lie,* he thought. *A total lie. But what is real? Perhaps I was alive when they died.*

"Carol. Didn't you say Tianna has been reincarnated six times?" He yelled.

"Yes, Harry. Why do you ask?"

Harry stood and approached the two. He sat down, looked at the plat map from 1904 and said, "If I was reincarnated I could have been alive when these people were killed and buried? Any reason it couldn't have happened? I could have killed them in a previous life and I came back to suffer for the sins of my past."

"Yes, and perhaps Roger was Queen Victoria during the Victorian age. I don't think so, but you never know."

Roger looked across the table. "Harry, I suggest you hold the questions of you having been alive in the 1880s until you talk to Tianna. I'm sure she can sense others who have been reincarnated like herself."

Harry mulled over the idea and said, "I suppose."

"I'm trying to analyze my situation as if it were a legal case. I know the memories or dreams controlled my life. I accept that my reality of the past was only my truth, but that reality was subjective. Also, in this lifetime, I didn't kill anyone."

Roger laughed, "Good. Perhaps you were one of the other dead, rising from the fire of 1887. Either way, get some rest. Carol and I will present our plan when Tianna arrives in the morning."

Harry walked around the table and eyed Carol's paperwork. He could see photographs mixed in with old copies of census forms. Carol turned toward him and smiled. "This," she pointed to the pile of papers, "is your life, Harry. The plan is to go day by day... staying with the flow... trying not to make a big show." She grinned. Roger laughed, and Harry turned toward his bedroom.

"Perhaps tonight I'll dream of burying the two of you," he warned.

***

Charlie rolled over. He sensed someone watching. His eyes roamed the dark motorhome. There, at the window... a man's silhouette... staring at him.

"Jonathon, what the hell is wrong with you?" he called out.

He heard nothing but the rustle of Jonathon in the bed next to him. The silhouette melted away and Charlie drifted back into his dream... only to be awoken by the sun streaming through the woods and into the window.

He checked his watch. *Six... Should I get up, roll over or... damn, I know... the bathroom, quick.*

Lila stepped aside and watched him rush into the room. Standing at the toilet, he turned and grinned. "It's going to be a good day. I can feel it."

"Oh yes, and I can see *IT*, too." Her eyes greeted him and returned a smile and a wink.

"Sorry, Lila. This is for someone special, hopefully Tianna." He reached over and ran water over his hands and asked, "What time did you throw John Boy out of bed?"

"Around midnight. You know, the witching hour."

Charlie faced her and realized she was almost naked. His face turned red, and he rushed out of the room, only to be stopped by Lila's hand on his arm.

"Listen, you little pervert. You don't hit on Tianna. You treat her like a queen or princess, not a sexual object. Let the romance happen on its own. It might never happen. Don't worry." Her hand twisted Charlie's arm. "Understand?"

Charlie nodded. "OK. Can I take a shower now? You can join me if you like."

Lila turned away, grinning, shut the door upon her exit, and saw Jonathon standing at the window. As she approached him, he faded and sat up on the edge of the couch.

"What do you want?" He could see Lila was in a daze. *She gets this way after a night of drinking and wild sex,* he thought.

"Lila, you look like you've seen a ghost." He held her shoulders and pulled her into his chest.

She inhaled and looked up. "I saw a ghost. My first one. I knew if I stayed at it long enough, I would eventually see one. Hey, Charlie. I saw a fucking ghost in the kitchen."

Charlie heard her words as he finished himself off in the

shower, cold water flowing over his back and neck. He turned the tap off. Reaching for the towel, his mind went to the man's silhouette in the window. *What do they want?* Then back to Tianna, the beautiful woman of his dreams.

CHAPTER 28

Rummaging through his belongings, pulling out clothes he'd seldom worn, his cell phone, and the leather organizer his wife gave him, Harry dressed, exited his bedroom, and greeted Roger and Carol at the table. "Well, don't we all look like a cheerful group of business people, getting ready to face the capitalist world?"

Carol laughed, "Harry, nice to see you're in a chipper mood." She wasn't familiar enough with the man to know about his moods. "The coffee is hot, the bagels are better toasted, and yes... this is a business meeting. Have you boys decided what you're going to say to the sheriff?"

Roger looked up from his notebook and turned to Harry, now standing next to Carol. "Well?" He smiled and sipped his coffee. "I think we can handle him."

Harry grinned like a Cheshire cat. "Shouldn't be a problem. I just hope the good sheriff doesn't turn this into a campaign trick. He is up for election, and he likes his job." Turning to Carol he asked, "Are the animals in their cages? Charlie looked frightful last night. Are you sure it's smart letting him live the lifestyle of Lila and Jonathon?"

Carol cut him off. "Yes, Harry, it's all under control. If the ghosts will let us, we will meet on the patio. It is a beautiful morning and I want to enjoy my visit." She pushed the door, turned back, and smiled at the two men she left standing at the table.

"Damn, Roger. You're my doctor, shouldn't you be doing

something about her?"

"I am. I'm putting some butter on my bagel."

Carol met Charlie at the patio table. Jonathon and Lila followed him; Jonathon had a large bag of what smelled like donuts.

"Here you go, Carol." Jonathon said. "I got up early and went to that bakery in Bad Axe, the Irish fellow, Murphy's. Yes, that's it. Are we going to be digging graves today? I didn't get the schedule, or perhaps my phone missed it."

He sat down and motioned for Lila to sit next to him. She walked past him and stood with Charlie, who was sipping coffee while holding a half eaten jelly-filled donut in his left hand. "Kid, you look great. No nerves or crazed ghosts this morning?"

"Thanks. No ghosts out here. There was one walking around in the motorhome this morning. You said you saw him when I was finishing in the shower. I'm not sure which one he was. Harry tried to identify them all for me, but they somehow appear as a haze or shadow. He could have been Farmer Bill."

"That's what I saw. A dark figure with backlighting. I thought it was Jonathon."

"So did I." Charlie smiled and turned to Carol. "Grandma... I mean Carol." He winked at Lila. "When is Tianna getting here, and are we doing any work on the graves and bones today?"

"No work for you, Charlie." Carol stood, moved toward Lila, and whispered to her, "Whatever you do, don't come on to the sheriff or anyone he brings with him today."

"Carol, that's cold. You know I'm better than that."

"Yes, but I keep remembering myself when I was your age, and now I'm just offering guidance. I know you, dear, and some men just turn you on like a wind-up doll. Besides, I'm your boss, so be good. That's an order."

"No problem, Carol. And be good too." Lila returned to be with Jonathon. She considered Carol's comment about the wind-up doll. *If anyone is a wind-up doll, it's Jonathon.* She put her arm around him, pretending to wind the key on his back.

"That feels good, he laughed."

Jonathon finished his doughnut and called to Carol, "Are you aware there is a road block a quarter mile down, at the corner. I had to do some fast talking to get back here. Even had to flash my FBI badge."

Roger heard the comment as he and Harry approached the group. "The sheriff said he was going to keep people out. He's doing a public statement to quell some rumors. People are always curious, and we don't want anyone messing with our graves."

When Harry and Roger found a seat, Carol raised her voice and spoke.

"Today is a big day for our investigation. Sheriff McNabb will be here in less than an hour, and Tianna Gulliver and Detective Lester Thornson will arrive a little after nine. It will be a busy morning and I want everyone to be on their best behavior."

Roger cleared his throat and spoke. "Carol, I trust your team will shine this morning. Harry and I will lead the conversation with the sheriff. We talked to him earlier, and he is aware of our graveyard, but he thinks the investigation is archaeological, not criminal. It is our intention to reinforce that idea and keep him somewhat in the dark. It is important that when you talk to McNabb and his people, you must not talk about ghosts or Harry's involvement, other than that he called us to investigate the graves that he accidentally dug up. That's our story, and we don't want it corrupted."

Roger turned to Harry. "Anything else?"

"Yes. Thank you for the kindness and understanding you have given me. This has been difficult for me. When I contacted Roger, I needed help and wanted to turn myself in as the killer of sixteen people. I knew I was on the edge of a mental breakdown." He turned to Roger, and through tears he added, "You have walked me through my personal hell and showed me the light at the end of my tunnel. Thank you. I am understanding the curse that was placed on my young shoulders, and with your help, the yokes of the past can be removed."

Roger smiled, "Well put, my friend."

Carol watched as two Huron County police cars turned into the driveway. "They are here. Let the circus begin."

CHAPTER 29

Sheriff McNabb, a man of huge stature, walked toward the team. His deputy, Ned Wooddell, followed him. The sheriff extended a hand out and said, "Harry, for a crazy old man, you're looking good. I take it the good doctor here has helped you?"

"He's done wonders. But let me introduce you to the team that is investigating the graveyard I found on Dad's old homestead."

"I noticed the graves. Any idea who they were?"

"I'll let Carol give you those answers. Sheriff, this is Carol Edmonds."

Carol approached. "Sir, I'm a forensic anthropologist from Ann Arbor, and this is my team of investigators. The FBI calls us whenever unknown human skeletal remains are found."

Lila and Jonathon inched forward as Carol continued, "This is Lila Budd, my assistant, and Jonathan Saunders, our resident FBI agent. Charlie, come here a minute."

Charlie pocketed his phone and approached; Carol continued, "And this young man is my grandson, Charles Rehnquist. Charlie is a student assistant."

McNabb shook everyone's hand and declared, "I'm glad to meet you all. Now, what is the status of this investigation? I will speak to the press in a few minutes. Nothing major, just the local paper and radio reporters."

Roger inched between the sheriff and Carol's team. "Sir, we brought the FBI in because this graveyard is unmarked and not registered anywhere in the history of Huron County. This led us to suspect possible foul play."

Carol injected, "Our investigation suggests that if it was a crime, it happened in the 1880s. We are working on trying to identify the bones, but because of their age, it is very difficult, and we are not expecting to reach any definitive conclusions."

"Excellent news. Harry, Roger, let's go talk to the press." The three men walked toward the county police cars, where there were now several people standing with Ned, the deputy sheriff. While they took questions from the reporters, Carol and the team returned to the patio table to talk about Tianna's arrival.

Harry put his hand on Roger's shoulder. "Cover for me. I think we have a big problem. The ghosts have gathered and they look angry."

Roger whispered, "Do what you can. We don't want them making waves while the sheriff is here."

"I know."

Roger excused Harry and took a question from the WLEW radio reporter as Harry rushed to the team on the patio. "Charlie, can we stop them?"

Charlie was watching the ghosts. "I'm not sure. Let's see if they will let us talk to them," he said, walking toward the ghosts.

Arnold, the old, tall ghost who was still in grave number sixteen, turned and looked as the two men approached them. "See, they are evil. They want to take our spirits and destroy us. Are we going to let them? Are we going to work together and stop them?"

"Lord yes," yelled old lady Clara. "Can we kill them, Arnold?"

"If we work together, no one can stop us."

Harry and Charlie listened to the threats. Charlie closed his eyes and tried to send a message. Nothing.

"I'm not getting through to them. What now?"

Harry looked back at the sheriff. "We have to stall. I think our visitors are ready to leave. Roger is doing everything he can to get them out of our yard."

Charlie turned and ran full force into the group of ghosts. He screamed, "Run... Run, you bastards. Run away."

They didn't and Charlie stopped, as if he had hit a brick wall. Harry rushed to him and heard a soft voice behind him. It was a beautiful young black woman. The ghosts scattered as she approached.

Tianna bent down and touched Charlie's face with her hand. She turned to Harry and said, "Sir, he's going to be fine, but those ghosts won't stop until we get to the root of their sorrow."

Charlie sat up and smiled. "You must be Tianna. I'm Charlie and I love you."

"You tell every girl that when you first meet them?" Tianna laughed and stood. She extended her hand and helped Charlie up. Sparks exploded and Tianna smiled. "Yes, Charlie, you do love me. I will tell you all about our love soon."

Harry watched as the sheriff and a muscular black man in his early sixties approached.

Sheriff McNabb bellowed, "What the hell happened here?"

"Charlie stumbled and Tianna helped him," Harry said. "I think he'll be fine. I keep telling the young man to be careful in these woods. There are a lot of fallen branches hidden by the leaves." He turned to Charlie and winked. "Will your ankle be OK?"

Charlie reached down and rubbed. "I think so. There doesn't seem to be any damage, other than to my pride, Sir."

Harry extended his hand out to Detective Lester Thornson. "Lester, it's good to see you again. What's it been, about ten years?"

"Probably more, but who counts years anymore?"

Harry guided the sheriff and Lester away from the woods as

the ghosts peeked out from behind the trees. "Well Sheriff, did the interview with the reporters go as you wanted?"

"Sure did. It surprised me that the FBI would involve a Detroit detective in this matter. Is there more here than meets my eye?"

"No," Lester replied. "I drove up so my friend and neighbor, Tianna Gulliver, could join this team. She is studying with Carol and needed a ride, and I wanted to visit with my old friend Harry so I took the day off."

It pleased Harry that Lester was working the story, avoiding the truth as much as possible. "Yes, Lester and I go back about ten years. I met him when I was representing Albert Doyle winning his case against the city of Detroit. What was that, ten years ago?"

The sheriff bellowed with laughter, "What a small world. I didn't know you knew Doyle. He's my rent-a-detective. He helped me with a murder case last year. Nice man, and a superb cook. Doyle makes the best damn cookies I've ever eaten."

Harry laughed, "I can't believe you eat cookies."

"Shut up, Harry. I know I'm fat, but I just love to eat. If I die from my diet, at least I'll die a happy man."

"Very good, Sir. By the way, you have my vote and if you need any advertising funds, let me know. I'll be glad to help." Harry paused. "Don't let that chin hit your belly. I'm serious, and I am better because of Roger's hard work, and these people. Carol's team will clear this place of any potential crimes from the past."

"Thank you, and we can talk about you helping my campaign later. Anything I can do to help with your investigation, just call." The sheriff turned and approached his car, where Deputy Ned was standing with Lila and Carol. The two girls, Harry suspected, were plying Ned with their wiles.

CHAPTER 30

Sheriff McNabb yelled to Carol, "Honey, you can't have my man. He's engaged, or at least getting serious with another woman."

Carol laughed. "Damn, Sheriff, Lila and I were looking to spend some quality time with this sweet man." She ran her hand down his side. "But we can take no for an answer. I trust you and Harry are good now. We will solve this mystery."

"Yes," Lila butted in, "We love mysteries, especially ones with old bones. They have so much to tell us."

"Sure, honey." The sheriff opened his door and crawled in as Ned said his goodbyes and walked to his car.

After the law officers left, Carol could breathe easier. "Harry, we have to keep these fucking ghosts from killing my grandson. I don't like the way this case is going. Where is he?"

"In the living room with Tianna... and Lester." Harry added Lester to calm Carol. "Charlie will be fine. You know he saved the day. I'm sure the ghosts were ready to attack the sheriff. Can't you see the headlines. Sheriff mysteriously assaulted by sixteen ghosts. The attack took place in Harry's graveyard, just south of Bad Axe."

"It would have been worse if we had to report his death."

"True." Harry took Carol's hand. "Come on, let's go into the house and talk with Tianna."

Lila was already at the house when Harry and Carol reached the door. "Harry, please kiss me and give me a big hug. I need it so bad."

126

Harry smiled, kissed and hugged the beautiful woman. His arms embraced her tense body, and he could feel her melting. Her lips sped up tempo and force, but he pulled away. "Save some for later, when I'm tense and need attention."

Carol laughed. "You tense? After all the crap you've lived through? I don't think that's tension, that's just being horny."

"Perhaps, but we have work to do." He kissed her again and opened the door for her.

Roger was working at the kitchen table. His eyes left the screen of his notebook, and he smiled. "You two look happy. Is it something I should know?"

"No, Roger," Carol cooed. "We were just having a moment outside. Where are Charlie and Tianna?"

"In the living room with Detective Thornson. She is a lovely young girl. Can she actually walk in the spirit world?"

"As I understand, yes. I have no proof, but I have talked to people who were with Tianna while she was in that realm. Perhaps she will demonstrate for us."

"Wouldn't that be nice," Harry injected. "I could use some excitement in my life. Let's go talk to the dead spirits."

Roger and Carol looked at each other and grinned. Carol said, "That's the idea, Harry. She can go back and relive the death of each of the ghosts in your graveyard."

Harry considered her words. "Yes, I can see what you mean. I hope she can do that."

Roger nodded his head in agreement. "Indeed. I trust the stories, but fake psychics are always backed up by satisfied customers, or believers."

Tianna and Lester were standing in the doorway, listening to the conversation. Carol was first to notice them. "I'm sorry, dear, we…"

Tianna interrupted her sentence, "I understand. It took my best friend, Amber, months before she realized it wasn't a magic trick. I will show my ability later." She hesitated. "Carol, can I talk to you in private?"

"Of course." She turned to Roger and Harry. "Guys, go into the living room; us girls need some alone time."

Lester announced he had to get back to Detroit, so he hugged Tianna. "Remember, if you need anything, just call. Amber wants you to call her this evening after you get settled in."

Tianna replied, "I will, and thank you for driving me here. I think I will enjoy working with Carol's team. Bye." Lester shook hands with everyone and slipped out the door.

When the men were out of range, Tianna approached Carol and said, "I need to spend some time alone with Charlie, and I need you to help."

"Of course, dear, but what is this about?"

"When we go into the realm, our bodies will be here in stasis. I need you to keep watch."

"Yes, but what is this all about? Why do you need to be alone with Charlie?"

"Depending on how Charlie reacts, I will tell you what I can after we return. Trust me. I need to take him somewhere special so we can talk."

Carol wished she knew the "where and why," but she agreed. The two women walked back to the living room, where everyone except Lila and Jonathon gathered.

Tianna touched Charlie's shoulder and whispered, "We're going to take a trip into the past. I asked your grandmother to cover for us."

Charlie stood up, wondering what she had planned. "The past? Is this going to be a sample of your abilities?"

"Yes, but there is something you need to know, and it will be easier to show you, than explain."

"I'm game. What now?"

"Carol, can you come with us for a moment?"

Carol approached, and together they walked into Harry's bedroom. Tianna continued, "Charlie, sit next to me on the bed. We'll hold hands and travel into the realm of the spirits while our bodies remain here. If I were my grandfather, we would sit around a fire in the shaman's hut. I learned a great deal from him during my first lifetime, in the 1690s."

Carol asked, "What is it I'm to be doing while you are on this trip?"

"Just make sure no one disturbs us."

The entire event excited Charlie, yet he had an uneasy feeling. *Where is she taking me? Why now, and why do I feel such an affinity toward her?* Questions that he wanted to ask, but didn't. Questions he was sure she would answer soon.

The two teenagers held hands and within seconds, Charlie opened his eyes. They were sitting in a birch hut with a fragrant fire burning in the center of the room. Across from them was an old Indian man, his hair decorated and spiked crazily.

He spoke in an ancient language, Algonquian. Somehow, Charlie could understand his words. "Arianna, it is good to see you again. Young man, you will learn something exciting about yourself today."

"Grandfather, I just met Charlie. He can walk with the spirits."

"I know. I can sense it. Charlie, as a young man you studied with me. You were on your way to becoming a great shaman, but your love for my granddaughter was unbearable. After her death, you became a great warrior and died in battle. I cried and prayed for you many nights."

Charlie tried to piece together the meaning. "I assume then that I lived here before?"

Tianna turned her attention to Charlie. Holding his hands and looking into his dark eyes, she said, "You were my brother's best friend. Even though we were the same age, I didn't return your affection. I was intent on showing my father what a great warrior I was. My mind became twisted by the love of a young French soldier, down in Fort Pontchartrain du Détroit. I was turning sixteen, and a rival Indian tribe attacked us, and I ran to be with my French lover, but they killed me. I saw you and my brother as my spirit was ascending. You were strong, handsome, and perhaps if I had chosen you, the guardians of the spirit realm could have allowed me to live. Instead, my spirit lifted into the heavens to be with our ancestors, only to repeat my journey five more times."

CHAPTER 31

Tianna was thorough in her handling of Charlie, leaving him on a limb with nowhere to climb or jump.

In the realm, the two walked down old Hastings Street where Tianna was Sarah Weinberg, a beautiful young girl living above the family deli during prohibition. She stopped in front of the deli and pointed to the old man in the window. That's my grandfather. He can't see us, but I love coming here to watch him. I love all of my former families.

Charlie was silent, considering everything that had happened in the past few hours. He took Tianna's hand and said. "I can see some of my memories returning. Was it difficult when you realized you had six previous lives?"

"Yes. It is still hard to grasp. Every time I step into the realm, I consider all that has happened in the past. The pain, the joy, the beauty, the horror. I'm sure when we walk with Harry's ghosts we will touch on all of those emotions, revealing the last moments of their past lives."

"Did I have over one life?"

"I'm not sure... perhaps."

Tianna picked up a newspaper blowing along the street. "Today's news."

Charlie read the headline. 'Another Purple Gang Killing' 'When Will It End!'

"Tianna, I still have powerful feelings for you. I am relieved I was your brother's friend and not your brother."

Laughing through her words, Tianna said, "So am I." She

turned and hugged Charlie. The hug was long, and Charlie didn't want it to end. Tianna pulled away. "I like you, too; perhaps we will become more, but from the lessons of my past, I know the importance of taking one's time. This is my last life; I have to make it count."

***

Carol was away from the bedroom for only five minutes when she heard Charlie's voice. She rushed back and hugged him. "Damn, I was afraid something bad happened." She turned to Tianna and asked, "Where did you take him?"

"Back to when we were kids. During my first life in 1690, Charlie was my brother's best friend. We both have the same heritage and now he understands why he sees the spirits, and he will become stronger and more powerful in his quests."

Carol stood. She was both shocked and surprised at Tianna's grasp on life. She was speechless. Charlie did a thumbs up for Tianna and smiled. He, too, was surprised at how graceful his new *old friend* was. He walked to the window. The west sun streamed through the blinds, into the room.

"Grandma, why don't we go to the living room and visit with Mr. Thornson."

Tianna concurred, and soon the visit to the realm was set aside. Charlie felt comfortable with his new realism and confident that during this lifetime he would embrace as his mate, the lovely Tianna. *First, I have to break some ties with Grandma. I'm eighteen. Carol doesn't need to watch my every move,* he thought.

"Charlie, stop thinking so much," came the familiar voice of Lila Budd.

Followed by the loud voice of Jonathon, "Lilly, what did you mean when you said Charlie was back from his trip?"

"John Boy, she means I've discovered that I can walk through time within the spirit world. Awesome. Isn't it? I just have to figure out how we did it." He looked around the room. "Tianna, tell me how."

Tianna smiled and approached him. "Indeed, how?"

After milling around the room, talking to everyone about the team, the plan, Charlie's new life, Harry's ghosts, Tianna's beautiful hair and chocolate skin, Lila's favorite positions, and Jonathon's favorite positions, Roger looked at Harry and said, "And you thought you were crazy?"

The two men walked into the kitchen. Harry reached in the refrigerator and pulled out another cold beer. "Yes, I thought I was crazy, and I thank you for saving my life."

"My friend, I have not saved your life yet; don't forget, the ghosts are still with us. I know you didn't kill them, but I don't understand why they manifested themselves in the first place and then manipulated you into becoming their guardian." Roger filled his wine glass and continued, "There is more happening here than we have been able to see. I hope Tianna and Charlie can find some answers tomorrow."

Harry sipped his beer. "I wish I could go with them. I almost feel responsible; like I should make this right."

"If they need you, they will ask. For now, let's just relax and enjoy this beautiful afternoon."

As he ended his sentence, Tianna entered the kitchen with Charlie in tow.

"Harry, Charlie said you have a list of the people buried in the cemetery. Could you go over it with us? It will help me understand who they are and what I can expect to see." She sat down next to him and motioned Charlie to sit next to her.

Roger opened his briefcase and handed Tianna a folder marked *The Dead*. "It's all here. The names, descriptions, probable cause of death, and the age Harry was when he buried them.

I should say he dreamed he buried them. They were buried long before Harry was born."

Tianna and Charlie studied the papers for several minutes. "Roger," Tianna asked, "Could you get us something to drink?"

Charlie laughed, "I'll take some of that wine."

"Like hell. Do you want to see your grandmother kill me?"

"No, I was joking. I'll have a beer. Root beer, or cola. Tianna, what would you like?"

"Just cold water with ice, if you have it."

Roger stood and got the youngsters their drinks.

Harry asked Tianna, "Do you have questions about the ghosts?"

Tianna looked up and answered, "Yes. When you look back at the dreams, who was the most influential of the ghosts? I mean, is there one ghost who stands out as the leader?"

Harry answered, "The Bad Axe woman was the most outspoken, but I almost think the last man I buried, Arnold, was very important. I remember the other ghosts standing around the grave as I dug the hole. They were weeping and consoling each other, like his death was the end of their world. That struck me. I was seventeen, and it was the last grave I dug before leaving for college."

Charlie injected, "We haven't exhumed his body yet."

"I think we'll start from the first and work through them in chronological order. That way we will get the complete story." Roger passed out the drinks, and Tianna asked, "Can I keep these papers for a while?"

He replied, "Of course. I have copies on the computer. What time do you want to start tomorrow?"

Tianna looked at Charlie. "What do you think, after breakfast, about nine?"

Everyone agreed, even Carol, who was standing in the living

room archway. "I think we should all get some sleep. It's been a busy day, and we need to be in tip-top shape tomorrow." She turned to the living room and called, "Lila, Jonathon, did you hear that? Get some sleep tonight. No staying up all night again. Everyone, we have a mission to complete, so it's goodnight to you all. Come with me, Tianna. Goodnight, Charlie."

She escorted Tianna upstairs while Charlie wistfully watched. He wished he were with her, but knew it would take time. Besides, he will be with Tianna all day tomorrow. Something to fill his dreams tonight.

CHAPTER 32

Charlie took a quick, cold shower, while Lila and Jonathon talked about the work they would do in the morning. When Charlie walked in, Lila began laughing. "Is that a gun under your towel, or are you just glad to see me?"

Embarrassed, Charlie sat down. "Lila, you're such a bitch. I guess the cold shower wasn't enough to dull the sword. But seeing you and John Boy is enough to put all thoughts of romance out of my mind."

Jonathon stood and approached Charlie. "Was Tianna what you expected?"

"Yes, and more. It's crazy that we were together in a previous life. If I play my cards right, I might end up in a relationship with her this time around."

"For that to happen, you'll have to control yourself. She's a very mature eighteen, and you are a young and stupid eighteen. If you're not careful, she'll make mincemeat out of you."

Lila slapped her hand on the table. "Shut up, Jonathon. You do not know what a woman wants. Charlie, just be yourself. Tianna appears to be very intelligent. She can see what a nice boy you are. And if she could put up with you when you were a young Indian boy, she'll put out for you now. Have fun and don't listen to Jonathon."

Jonathon grabbed a beer and walked outside. Lila didn't follow him. Instead, she went to the bedroom and locked the door. Charlie stretched out on the sofa bed and checked his phone. There was a message from his friend Elizabeth. "Are you

136

and Tianna an item yet?"

He messaged back, "Liz, I'm working on it. I have a story that will put you on your ass. During the 1700s I was an Indian warrior, and I died at Fort Pontchartrain. I've had a three-hundred-year crush on that girl. It's crazy, but true."

Elizabeth wasn't online, so the message went unread. Charlie drifted off to dreamland, only to be awakened by the horrific scream of Jonathon in the backyard. He jumped up, put on his shorts, and ran outside. The moon was bright enough that he could see Jonathon writhing on the ground with the ghosts surrounding him.

With Lila at his back and Harry running from the house, he reached Jonathon first, grabbed him, and the old woman hit him. She screamed, "Get out of here, you bastards. We've had enough. Stop destroying our world."

Harry rushed to help his friends and watched the ghosts as they approached him. He screamed, "Stop. Stop this madness."

The ghosts halted and seemed surprised that their Harry would talk to them in this manner. Nine-year-old Casandra put her one arm out to touch Harry, but he slapped her hand in anger and yelled, "Leave me alone. Go away and leave me alone, Casandra."

The Bad Axe woman pulled Casandra away. They were both in tears as they dissolved into the mist.

Tianna approached Charlie and offered a hand, while Lila and Carol tended to Jonathon. Lila was in tears and she clung to Jonathon, holding him up. "You ass, what did you do to anger them?"

"Nothing. I was sitting with my feet dangling in the grave, smoking a cigar, when I felt something hit my face. I got up and tried to run to the house, but they... like Charlie described it, they raped me. Ran right through my body like a knife slicing butter."

"Hurts like hell, doesn't it?" asked Charlie as Tianna walked him to a patio chair.

She checked to make sure he wasn't bleeding and said, "These ghosts are not typical, are they?"

"No," replied Carol, walking with Lila and Jonathon. "They manifest themselves as a group and as a team they seem to have more power to inflict harm on us. We need to find the source of their power."

"Tianna and I will try to find the answers to those questions tomorrow," Charlie said.

Tianna added, "We are starting with the babies and Casandra. By following them in the order they died, we should be able to piece together the events covering the timeline of the graveyard."

"Excellent," replied Carol. "Are you going to be OK?" she asked Charlie.

"Yes."

Jonathon interjected, "I'm OK too, Carol. The ghosts can inflict pain, but there doesn't seem to be any permanent damage."

Roger was making notes in his notebook and suggested everyone try to get some sleep. They all agreed and headed back to their bedroom. Harry watched as the ghosts stood at the edge of the woods. Casandra was still crying, and Caseville Man was throwing daggers with his eyes. *Everything is back to normal*, he thought.

***

Charlie rolled over and checked the time. Five past six. He stretched and tried to go back to sleep. He flinched as he felt something touch his thigh. His eyes opened, and there was a young girl looking down at him. He froze, not with fear, but so as not to startle her. She continued touching him, becoming more adventurous.

This is unreal, he thought. She's feeling me up. Am I dreaming?

A smile ran across the girl's face. Charlie wondered if she could hear him. "What's your name?" he whispered.

Her eyes met his, and he thought she said, "Cora."

She removed her hand and dissolved into a mist. Jonathon rolled over, coughed, and went back to sleep. Lila opened her bedroom door and walked through the kitchen wearing a skimpy negligée.

"Guess what, Lila," Charlie said.

"You have morning wood?" She smiled and grabbed a glass of water.

"Yes, but Cora, the young ghost, was here feeling me up. How crazy is that?"

"I'm sure you were just dreaming; why would she want to touch you?"

"I don't know, but she did." Charlie grabbed his shorts and slid them on under the covers. He stood and headed for the bathroom. "I could feel her touching me and she told me her name. I can't wait to see what Tianna and I discover today."

Jonathon woke and crawled out of bed. "Lila, you want a little fun before we get up?"

"No," she said. "I'm not interested. Perhaps one of the ghosts will help you out. Charlie said one of them tried to feel him up. I'm sure he was dreaming, but who knows? Perhaps ghosts get horny too." She giggled at the thought and returned to her room.

By eight o'clock, the entire team had gathered around the kitchen table. Lila made pancake batter as Carol fried eggs and bacon on the stove. The coffee was hot, and the table was set.

Roger put his notebook away and asked Harry if he had a good night.

"Yes, I slept well. No dreams, no ghosts, just restful sleep. You?"

"Same, but I understand Charlie had an unusual encounter with Cora. Something about her becoming amorous with him." The tone of his voice irritated Charlie.

"It wasn't a dream. She was coming on to me."

Tianna smiled. "It happens. I've had several ghosts try to get romantic. You have to swat them away like flies." She broke out laughing. "I'm sorry. It's just so funny."

CHAPTER 33

As the breakfast table was cleared, the conversation centered on Tianna and Charlie's trip into the realm. Harry asked if he could accompany the teens, and Carol squashed the idea.

"Tianna and I went over her plan, Harry. All you have to do is spend time this morning telling her about the first four people buried in the graveyard. We are going to follow your list, but we need background information. Tianna said she can find the timeline if we can make an educated guess when they died."

Tianna cleared her throat and said, "Yes, as long as we are less than a year from the actual time of burial, I can scan the period. We will start at the gravesite, and when we have the burial, I can follow the deceased back to his or her death. Their death details are what we will want to observe."

Harry understood what Tianna was talking about. The *time*. That point when the event that changed his life happened. The moment when the spirits took him into their fold. Actual time.

Tianna could travel in time like no other human. A master of the universe of time, human, female, and now very alive, she knew life and death because she experienced both. She caught Charlie off guard when she told him she was the Indian princess, Arianna. He was in love with her, and they lived in the Huron Indians' village, some three hundred years ago.

Knowing that the woman of his dreams was real, Charlie embraced his new reality. The dreams of his youth now had a new meaning, allowing him to become comfortable with him-

141

self. He wondered, *She is real and now she is Tianna. She was and still is the love of my life, but she... she could control my life if I let her.*

"Harry," Tianna asked, "could we spend an hour alone? I want to memorize the list of the ghosts Charlie and I will be observing. I need you to paint a mental image of each of them for me."

It surprised her that Harry didn't respond. He just sat there, thinking. Then, "It will be difficult, but if I keep it brief, I should be able to. However, shouldn't Charlie be here with us? You are both going into the realm, aren't you?"

Tianna smiled. "Yes, I'm sorry. I am used to doing this alone or with my friends back in Detroit."

She approached Charlie. "I wish we had more time to get acquainted before we're jumping into the past. If you will tolerate me, I guess we can learn together. You can join Harry and I for this lesson."

The look on Charlie's face was... doubt.

Tianna offered, "You can help me remember everything Harry tells us."

Charlie's expression was now blank. In desperation, she took Charlie's arm and led him into the kitchen like a child. Charlie turned and freed his arm, stepped back, and said... "Look. I know these fucking ghosts, and if you can't see that, then you know nothing about me or ghosts."

With an enormous smile on her face, her feet apart, and arms on her hips, she leaned forward and whispered, "Thanks for showing up, Charlie. I knew YOU were someplace in that *wonder* mind of yours. When we are in the realm, I need to trust your instincts. That means you have to be open and honest with me."

She leaned back and put her hands out. "Now we can work together. Just remember, what I say goes... at least while we are in the realm."

"Why? I thought you need to trust me?"

"I do, but I also need to lead. Being in the realm is complicated. We cannot alter anything, or we could alter the present and that would lead to a tragedy. The only reason I'm allowed to go into the realm of the spirits is because I have shown that I can follow the rules. If I do something wrong, it could lead to my death, and perhaps yours.

"I understand, but does this mean you will never trust me enough to follow my lead?"

"Charlie, that level of trust must be earned. In time... I am sure I will trust you as I am asking you to trust me."

"Agreed. I remember my Indian traits from our first life. Your grandfather was a wonderful man; I can learn from you, as he taught you the ways to the past and its connection to the future."

Tianna grew agitated and circled Charlie. "You have grown into a remarkable man. But you sideline me. Our mission is to help Harry release his ghosts so that they are returned to their families and placed into God's hands. We will talk about our past, later. Let's get back to Harry. We have work to do before we leave."

Charlie bowed and gestured toward the door. "After you, My Princess."

She smiled and walked. He laughed and said, "It will be a glorious future," and followed.

***

Harry put his cup on the table and pulled a chair next to Roger, who turned and smiled. "Have you gone over the grave information with Tianna?"

Harry sipped his coffee and blew across it to cool the surface.

"No. She and Charlie have to work out their details first. The electricity between them is amazing."

Roger chuckled. "Carol told me that as well. She is monitoring their progress. I understand she traveled into the realm with Tianna last night. It would be fascinating to go there."

Harry agreed. "I had hoped Tianna would ask me to join her and Charlie, but I think she's afraid of how I might react to the events they are studying."

Roger fell into his doctor mode. "Yes, that's likely why, but there could be other reasons. You might influence her through your reactions to the events. After all, you have history with these spirits, and that history might disrupt or alter the past."

Indeed, Harry thought. *A life of evil history, a life of...*

Tianna and Charlie entered the kitchen. "Can we go to the living room to talk?" She didn't wait for the answer, and turned back to Charlie. "Let's go to the couch. There is a fireplace, and I told Carol to start a small fire."

She motioned Charlie to sit in the large recliner. "Roger, let Harry sit here next to me, and you can sit next to him."

The two men, sitting to her left, and Charlie at her right; she began. "Charlie and I have agreed to work together to solve this mystery. Harry, the two babies died the same year, and Carol and Lila didn't see any cause of death indications."

She walked toward Harry and knelt on her knee. "Give me your hand."

Harry felt a sudden chill as the wind caught his face. "Where am I?" He turned around and realized he was outside his house, but the backyard changed. The house changed. No graveyard. Just a clearing, surrounded by woods.

"How old am I?" he questioned.

"Harry, you're ten years old, but we have to go back, NOW."

The chill again and the feel of a breeze. "That is hard to

believe," he said.

Roger looked surprised. "Harry, Tianna just wanted to hold your hand. What's not to believe about that?"

Tianna continued to hold Harry's hand. Looking into his eyes, she continued, "That is why I can't take you into the realm. I now see that they connected you to the past, and if I take you there, you could cause a change in the fabric of time. And that is dangerous."

Harry understood. "Why am I connected to the realm if I never buried them?"

Tianna sighed and stood. She sat on the arm of Charlie's chair and crossed her legs. Her stretchy jeans glimmered and Charlie noticed. A stirring started, and he tried to listen. *Move the mind away from desire... and embarrassment.* He thought for a moment and then stood to adjust himself.

Tianna watched as he sat down next to Roger. Charlie asked, "Why weren't you afraid of that happening when I was with you in the Indian village. I was alive then, but that didn't cause any problem. Why?"

With a grin she said, "Because I took you to a time before we were born. Having never been there, we couldn't get caught in the stream of our own lives. When you learn to control your skills in the realm, you can visit your own past."

Harry laughed out loud. "Now that we all know why I can't go, let's get back to the task at hand. I only remember putting the two small boxes in the ground... for... babies." Tears flooded his eyes. "I couldn't imagine what monster I was if I had killed them." A deep breath to relax. "It was a troubling time."

Roger continued taking notes. He looked up as Tianna stood. His eyes on her alone, he said. "I'm going outside to talk with Carol. You three can handle the details here."

"Thank you," Charlie, Tianna, and Harry said in unison. They laughed and watched Roger exit.

Harry continued, "Casandra lost an arm and half of her face. She was a wonderful nine-year-old girl. I believed she was my first kill." Harry took a deep breath. "I had to put her in a box and bury her as deep as I could. It wasn't really deep because the ground was cold... frozen... perhaps. I think it was January."

Tianna thought for a moment, then asked, "Why do you call her a wonderful girl? That implies you may have known her before she died."

"No. I didn't know her then. Over the years her ghost came to me comfortingly, as if trying to help me. I believe these ghosts have compassion, and Casandra was almost like a friend to me. I remember her sitting in my room when I was ten and talking. We almost became playmates. She might have been more because I was entering puberty and filled with emotions and feelings, and my memories are filled with the evil dreams."

Charlie injected, "A little compassion and a lot of anger. Harry, they are waging war against us; they don't want to be removed from this place. They may love you, but they hate us."

"I agree," responded Tianna. "Clara is the fourth person we will be tracking. It says on this list that you call her the Bad Axe woman. Why?"

Harry leaned forward on the edge of the couch and sighed. "When I buried her, she was such an old woman. Then, after I started seeing ghosts, I realized she was so big, strong, and not so old. The Bad Axe woman was a leader, along with Farmer Bill. I don't know if they are lovers or sister and brother, but they are always together. There is a bond between them."

Tianna wanted more details, but settled for Harry's memories. It was obvious Harry didn't know them before they died.

"Charlie, I think we have enough. Do you have questions to ask?"

"No, we've covered everything. I can offer information on

my interactions with the ghosts, but I, like Harry, have nothing on their pre-death lives."

***

The two travelers are placed in a secure room, a circle of sorts. Perhaps like one used by a shaman from many years ago, or... even... my grandfather, Tianna thought, as she prepared for the journey into the past.

"Charlie, you may get seasick as we float through the fabric of time, in search of our estimated location and time." She said, "That part goes by quick, but the closer we get... the more intense the ride."

"Don't worry. I'm a good passenger and quite excited." He smiled.

They held hands and began moving in time... in search of Harry's ghosts.

Harry approached the door with fear on his face. Roger grabbed his arm and held him at bay.

"You can't stop them, Harry. They will find out what happened."

CHAPTER 34

Charlie wasn't prepared. He found himself at the helm of a flying ship or *runabout*, speeding through time, watching a streaming array of images in strands like DNA. He screamed, "Shit. Tianna, what the fuck did you do? I thought you wanted to help."

She sped off. He grew more frightened, but an enhanced awareness flooded his body, and he could see Tianna speeding ahead. He leaned to the right and back to the left. They were circling a 1966 A&W drive-in. Tianna slowed down and pulled up to Charlie. She motioned to pull over; they stopped outside a farm just north of the diner.

Charlie wanted to yell at her, but he didn't. It was obvious he needed initiation to the club and a lesson.

"You're not angry?" Tianna puzzled, "I thought you would want to kill me for throwing you into the realm, alone like that."

"I did, but I needed to get in control, so I had to use the fear I experienced during my first life." He looked out at the array of images... flowing... as if an endless reel of film. Images that he could jump into and investigate, like the farm field they were standing in. He marveled at the huge wooden barn and watched the antique cars driving on the two lane M-53 highway.

"You realize you've been here before, don't you, Sir?"

Charlie questioned the remark, "Sir?"

"Yes, Sir." She looked away in a trance... afraid of her feelings. "I lied when I said you only had one life." She turned back to see his reaction.

Memories flashed through Charlie's mind as he traced each moment for clues to the puzzle Tianna just created.

Charlie spoke, "From your use of the salutation, Sir, I assume I was once someone you respected. I just hope you will not tell me there is now a chance that we will never be together. I don't think I could stand that." he paused. "But... hey... you're the boss. Right?"

He turned away from her. Searching his memories. Frozen in the zone.

Tianna fought her inner fears and said, "Look, I like you... enough to think about love on some levels. Perhaps it is destiny for us to be together throughout our many lives, but it's taken this last moment to bring us together. I don't know, perhaps I will have to talk to all of my grandfathers. Damn it, Charlie. Your grandma, Carol, told me you were special; now I know why."

Charlie leaned in, placed his arms around her for a hug. He didn't expect her to reach out and pull his mouth onto hers. Her kiss sent shivers down his spine and made him tingle with excitement. The kiss lasted... as they each experienced euphoria. Tasting each other's lips, mouth, and breath.

Charlie was first to pull back. "Look, I know we're on a mission and time is relative." He chuckled, and she smiled. "Just tell me who I was."

Tianna hopped on her runabout and smiled. You were born in the mid-1650s and were a great Algonquin Indian chief and warrior who led our people through wars and into this great region of the lakes. You died at a young age and became immortal to all Huron tribesmen.

"And then I was reborn as your brother's best friend, a warrior again." Charlie remembered.

"Yes. Throughout the years that followed, we were reborn together, but our paths crossed only a few times. You were once a great jazz player on Hastings Street. My friends and I would sneak out and listen to your band. You were in so many of my private dreams."

Charlie questioned, "Will I remember all my previous lives?"

"You should. I did and still do, but you will have to work to keep them in their place. If you let your mind wander down the trail of the past, you can become consumed with it. Try to remember segments, remember with fondness, always remember that the future is where we are headed. The past is where we are coming from. Our mission is to fix the present so Harry can emerge from his past, and we can free his ghosts."

Charlie climbed onto his runabout. He studied the ship and thought. *I know where I've seen these, they're a fucking Sea-Doo.*

"Tianna, what's with these Sea-Doo things. I remember, some four hundred years ago, I was in the realm riding on the back of a cougar. Now that is a crazy memory."

Tianna looked up and smiled. "Yep, some memory. We don't need any mode of travel. I like the water and the Sea-Doo looked fun. If you prefer, we can just stream ourselves, like a human essence in the flow of time."

"Sure, I knew that. Can I bring back my cougar to ride?"

"Shut up, Sir. How do you expect me to calculate the time of Casandra's death?"

The cougar doesn't eat much, and he never got in the way. And... shit... that's a dumb idea. I guess when you're alone and a crazed Indian warrior, you become one with the animals, both for food and comfort. Charlie was so glad he didn't stream that memory to Tianna.

He studied her glimmering tight jeans, the motorbike vest over an abstract tee shirt, and the tennis shoes, almost like platform high heels.

She was scanning on her mobile device when she looked up and asked, "What's got your attention, Sir?"

"I think I'm understanding how much work I'll have in sorting all of this new data coming into my mind. If I were a computer program, it might be easier, but."

"Handle it like you would if you were a computer program. Sort, file, set keys, notes and tags. Some people like numbers; I prefer images as reminders or scents, tastes, and textures."

Tianna approached Charlie and showed him her phone. "We are in Bad Axe during 1966. We need to go a mile or so south and find the farmhouse during 1870. Probably in January."

Charlie jumped on the runabout. "Let's get there. The sooner we get this done, the sooner we can move on."

The two slowly rode through larger images... some weeks-long and others a month or two. *This,* Tianna thought, *is the part that makes me sea-sick. Here I am breaking down doors, running though homes and people's lives like a police officer trying to find a drug dealer in a high rise building.*

I agree, Tianna, but we have to do it. Sometimes the past gets fucked up and someone has to go fix it. We have to keep our timeline from breaking.

Tianna was amazed. *When did you start running through my mind, and why do I hear your thoughts?*

What happened to the... Sir?

Keep in my mind and I'll show you what Sir means, Sir.

OK. Sorry. I can't read your thoughts. When you direct a thought at me, I can hear it. It's more like a two-way radio or cell phone. We can use our imaginary electrical headset and we don't have to speak the words, just think the words. Charlie considered his words and wondered.

Tianna began laughing and turned left through a snowstorm. There was a small path surrounded by woods and half open fields. Rubble from the look of it. *Charlie, we're almost there.*

I'm going to bump ahead to get out of this storm.

A sudden stop brought a bright blue sky and white sparkling snow blanketing the path and fields. *Look,* he pointed to his left. *Isn't that Harry's house down that path?*

Tianna forcibly said, "Let's only use those imaginary head-phones of yours when we can't hear each other or don't want someone else to hear. I prefer to hear the words with my ears. More nuances. Sexier, too."

"Yes, Sir." Charlie smiled. "Should we walk or drive?"

"Run," she said as she bolted down the path. Charlie was on her tail and almost caught her as he slid in the snow... through her legs. She landed on his back and together they slid into the tree outside the house.

"This isn't Harry's house, is it?" Tianna asked.

"Yes, I've been there and here. Harry told us the original house burned down and a farmer built another house on the foundation. I think that was after the fire of 1871."

The two walked around the yard. There was a well pump, and a small wooden building. Charlie opened the door, put his head in, and quickly removed it with a look of disgust. "Damn, that stinks."

"Most out-houses do." Tianna walked into the clearing that was in the backyard. She knelt down and touched the earth where Casandra's grave should be.

"Well, is she there?"

"Not yet." Tianna smiled as her runabout appeared behind her. She jumped into the seat and circled around Charlie. "We need to bump into the future. This will get intense; it's a week at a time. I just look for keys, spikes, or missing data... clues."

Charlie jumped onto his runabout, which now had a cougar's image across the front and sides.

"Let's find the solution to this puzzle."

CHAPTER 35

Tianna and Charlie grew closer to the burial of Casandra, so Tianna slowed her pace. She bent down and touched the ground again. "That's odd. She's in the grave now, but there is no record of the burial."

"What do you mean?"

"There is a gap, missing data, and that's not a good sign."

Charlie slipped ahead and then back through the time.

"I see what you mean. Any idea what happened to the data?"

"No, let's push back and see how Casandra died. This isn't my favorite activity, but we have to know."

As night turned into day and back to night the two walked outside the farmhouse, and a girl's scream came from inside. Tianna walked through the door and slipped in, followed by Charlie. "Don't worry, they can't see us."

A tall, stocky woman, perhaps in her late fifties, towered over a young girl. "Casandra, you don't need to get upset. I'm sure Arnold didn't mean to hurt you."

"Grandma, I hate it here. Why can't I go live with my dad?"

"You know why, dear. We've talked about this before. Your father isn't capable of taking care of a young girl. That's why you're here. Arnold is letting us live here and all he expects is that you respect him. He is the head of this household, and you must do as he says."

"I hate him! I hate you! I wish I was dead!" Casandra yelled, as she grabbed a tattered shirt and ran out the door. She crashed into a large man as he came up the steps. She almost knocked him off the porch and ran into the woods.

"Get back here, young girl," he yelled and turned to the woman. "Clara, what's got into that girl now?"

"Arnold, it's the same thing as always. She hates you and me and she still wants to live with her dad."

"Do you want me to follow her? I think she needs the back of my hand to break down some of that rebellious nature. God knows, she is wild. Full of the devil."

"No. She'll be back when she gets too cold, and besides, hitting her won't help."

Charlie and Tianna walked out and followed Casandra's trail into the woods. She was wandering in circles, following a small creek. Charlie spotted her first, sitting on a fallen log while eating some dry bread she found in her pocket.

"I wish we could hear her thoughts. Poor girl looks so lonely," Tianna said. "Listen, someone else is in these woods."

They listened. Casandra also heard the rustling, jumped up, and ran. A large cougar bolted after her and pounced on the young girl. Tianna screamed and Charlie ran toward the carnage unfolding before his eyes and tried to grab the girl, but his hands and arms passed through them. He could not do anything but watch the cougar sink its fangs into Casandra's arm and face. Blood was everywhere, turning the crystalline snow into a red carpet of death.

Tears flooded both his and Tianna's eyes. He put his arm around her. "We knew she died violently; now we know how."

"I know, but it still hurts. I wonder how long it will take for someone to find her body?"

"I'm not sure, but I can't just stand here looking at her. Let's bump into the future and find out who discovers her."

There were sounds of men and women calling, "Casandra,

Casandra, where are you?" Soon a young man in his twenties ran up and fell to his knees. "Over here." He brushed snow off her blood-soaked body and screamed, "She's dead. Oh God, she's dead. Oh, God. Arnold. Come quick... she's dead."

Arnold knelt beside the teen. "Jimmy, give me your coat." He rolled Casandra onto the heavy canvas coat and bundled her in it. He hoisted the dead girl over his broad shoulder and stood.

Clara approached him. Between sobs she asked, "What killed her? A wolf or cougar?"

"Cougar." He pointed to the large cat tracks. "Clara, it was an accident. It's not our fault. We did the best we could for her."

Charlie and Tianna watched them walk back to the farmhouse. Arnold placed Casandra on a blanket in the parlor. Arnold's funeral service was ripe with praises to God and himself, the pastor. His words struck Charlie as prophetic: "You are all my children, and even when you die, you will forever be with me. Amen."

"Amen." the congregation of family and neighbors repeated. Tianna wrote in her phone notes, *Casandra died January, 15th, 1870. The burial was not visible because of missing data.*

She and Charlie slipped into the future to find the two babies who were about to die within a few months.

***

Charlie removed the cougar image on his runabout, returning it back to the original sea-doo. He suggested to himself that it would be better for Tianna's sake, but it was for his own reasons.

The trip back was brief; they were at the farmhouse within minutes, having covered two months in historical time. Tianna bent and touched the earth of Baby One's gravesite. Again, the body was there, but there was no data for the burial.

"This is making me nervous. I just hope the guardians of the realm don't think I am corrupting the time stream."

"How could you?" Charlie asked.

"I don't know, but they warned me about this and it makes me nervous."

Charlie felt the ground, walked back and forth through the time signature, and agreed with her. "Can you call the Guardians and ask?"

"I don't think they accept phone calls. I could ask Grandfather."

"Great. Let's call him." Charlie pulled his phone from his pocket and smiled. "I take it we won't use the phone to call him, right?"

Tianna smiled as a hand landed on Charlie's shoulder. With a start, Charlie turned and saw the Huron Indian Shaman standing behind him. "Sir," he stuttered, "You... surprised... me."

The brightly dressed Indian, with spiked long hair and paint splashed on his face, smiled. "My dress or my presence startles you, son?"

"Yes," Charlie said.

"Grandfather," Tianna said as she hugged him. She stood back and added, "We have a problem. The timeline seems to have missing data, and we're afraid the Guardians may accuse me of doing something wrong."

The two discussed the situation and moved back and forth through the burial period.

"Arianna, or should I call you Tianna?"

"Your choice."

"Well, don't worry about the missing data. I will speak to the Guardians and have them help you fix the issue." He turned to Charlie. "It is nice to see you again. I am sure you and my granddaughter will make a great team."

"Thank you. Now that I know and understand my past,

everything in my present life is becoming clearer. I, too, think Tianna and I will make a great team. But I know now that it takes time to bring us together."

Tianna laughed. "Time. Grandfather, we have to go. Thank you for easing my mind."

Tianna's grandfather dissolved into a mist, and she and Charlie climbed onto their runabouts. In a few seconds, they saw Arnold and Clara running from the farmhouse. Arnold ran to the small barn and returned with a buggy and a beautiful horse. Clara jumped into the buggy, and they sped down the icy path. About a mile away from the farm, they turned into another wooded area, and followed a snow-covered path covered with horse, buggy, and human prints. Arnold's buggy stopped outside a small log cabin.

The door was thrown open, and a young man, Jimmy, helped Clara down. She brought in her leather bag and ran through the door.

"Everyone who isn't having a baby, get outside. NOW!" Yelled Clara.

Charlie and Tianna watched as seven children and adults walked out of the small cabin.

Clara rushed to the bed where Anna, a very pregnant young woman, cried in pain.

Clara looked under the blanket as Jimmy and Arnold stood watching. Jimmy was holding Anna's hand, and Arnold paced back and forth.

Clara sighed. "It's too early, Anna. You shouldn't be delivering for weeks, and I have this awful feeling you might have twins."

"Twins," yelled Jimmy. "Why didn't you tell us that before?"

Arnold turned to the young man and scolded, "Don't you talk to her like that, boy. She's here to help your wife."

"Sorry," cowered the young man.

"I didn't know, Jimmy. I didn't know. But now, Anna, you need to push. The baby's head is almost ready to crest. Push through the pain."

Anna struggled through the agonizing pain and delivered the baby. There was silence as Clara tried to revive the tiny creature in her hands. Anna's eyes were glued to her. She screamed, "Why don't I hear my baby."

Clara bundled the body in a small piece of fabric and said, "Honey, your baby girl was stillborn, but you have another child that you have to concentrate on. You need to think about saving the next baby, do you understand?"

Anna was crying and reaching for the dead child, but Arnold took it from Clara and walked to the door. He turned to Jimmy and asked, "What name do you want on your daughter's grave?"

Jimmy looked at his wife for an answer. Through tears she uttered, "Mary."

"I will prepare a box, and we will bury the child next to Casandra on the farm. Clara, send Jimmy when you have the second child, and I will return with the buggy." He walked out with the bundle under his arm.

Tianna turned to Charlie. "Let's bump ahead and see the birth of the next child. I have a feeling it might also be stillborn."

Charlie agreed, and they carefully moved through the next few hours. A tiny boy was born; there was no sound until Clara worked her magic. The baby uttered a small cry, and Anna and Jimmy became overjoyed. Anna held her child and declared the boy would be named Marshall.

Charlie asked, "Now what?"

Tianna had a puzzled look on her face. "I don't know. Is the second baby, Marshall, or is it another baby boy?"

"I think we should go back to the graves and see when the second baby shows up; then we can re-examine our options."

In a matter of minutes, the couple were in the backyard. Tianna touched the ground. The baby was there, so they moved back through time. Again, the burial data was missing. They watched the farmhouse for clues. Moment by moment, they jumped back and stopped when they saw Jimmy riding an older horse down the path. He tied the horse to a fence post and ran into the house.

Tianna ran toward the house and passed through the door. Anna was holding her child, weeping uncontrollably as Jimmy rushed to her side.

"He's dead," she cried out. "My baby boy is dead."

Clara and Arnold stood side by side; their faces sullen. Clara said, "Jimmy, the child's lungs were too weak. He was born too early, and I couldn't help him recover. I am so sorry." Jimmy cried as he took his son into his arms and tried to hug his wife.

Anna walked away, turned, and screamed. "It's over. I never want another child. I can't handle this, Jimmy. It's over."

Jimmy handed his dead son to Arnold and ran after Anna. The couple argued and Anna crouched in a corner and wept. She wouldn't let him touch her.

Charlie asked Tianna, "Do we have to stay? We know what happened, right?"

"Yes, we can go. It is hard to see people at their lowest point in life, isn't it?"

Charlie blinked and opened his eyes. He was still holding hands with Tianna in the bedroom. He smiled and said, "That was exciting. Almost as exciting as being here alone with you."

Tianna chuckled. "Yes, but we don't have time for us, we have to talk to the team."

CHAPTER 36

Carol heard the two teens talking and opened the door. She stepped into the room and shut the door behind her. "You're back. Should we talk first, or do you want to share with all the team?"

Tianna stood and approached the team leader. "Carol, we had a productive trip into the realm. I think we can share with everyone."

Carol opened the door and as she stepped into the living room, she announced, "Everyone in the kitchen, now."

Roger and Harry were still at the table, talking. Lila and Jonathon heard Carol's call from outside and entered through the back door. Carol, Tianna, and Charlie walked into the room and stood with their backs against the counter.

Roger spoke up. "Well, Carol, I see our travelers have returned from their mission."

Harry had an uneasy feeling in his gut. The fears of his past deeds crept up on him again. He pushed back and said, "So, tell us what the verdict is. Guilty?"

Charlie laughed at his friend. "Only if we find out who stole the burial data. Harry, did you change the past?"

"Charlie, stop picking on him," Tianna scolded. "We found the cause for the babies' and Casandra's deaths. Accident, and premature twins. There is data missing for the burial. We can't see them being buried. The Guardians are going to be working with us to find out why."

Roger softly spoke. "It sounds to me like a rip in time. Is that why they are involved?"

Tianna nodded, and Charlie spoke. "It could be related to why these sixteen ghosts have been trapped in this timeline. If we solve the puzzle, we will rip them from this realm... into their family realm. To the light, so to speak."

Everyone laughed. Clara glared through the window with the hate of God in her heart. She turned and walked into the woods. Harry noticed her, Tianna saw her, Charlie felt her energy. He felt that energy when it blew through his body like a lightning strike.

Carol started to speak, but Harry interrupted with, "Kids. Do you have the energy to go back and finish this ordeal? Everyone is on edge, both us and the ghosts. The faster we can get there, the better for all of us. I don't know how long I can keep them at bay. They are a part of me, and I don't know how."

Roger understood. He put his arm around Harry and helped him to his seat. Harry became embarrassed; he gathered himself and straightened his back. "I am serious, I am caught up in this web of mine and I know God wants us to bring the love back and set these ghosts and people FREE."

***

Charlie and Tianna returned to the realm, weaving through time on their water-toys. Charlie was in his mind, amid thoughts of his past lives. He smiled as he watched Tianna swish and sway. Damn *such form.*

"Hey Tianna, did you lose your way?" he smiled.

"No. My mind was also astray."

Tianna was a little pissed. She wasn't used to having someone who could communicate on a mind-wave. She spoke. "Charlie, put your mind on the task, please. I want to get our jobs done."

Then we can go astray... She didn't say.

Spirals wrapped as two strands with streaming images, each a point in time. He laughed to himself. *Reminds me of a super highway with real-life stories along the way.*

Tianna screeched on her brakes; Charlie avoided hitting her. She stopped and scanned the data for a feeling she caught as they passed through the time.

"What is it?"

"I'm not sure, but it felt like Harry's vibration was here. I was looking back to see what age he was." She turned and stared into the realm, thinking of her grandfather and her father, who lead as the chief of his kingdom. One was the leader, and the elder was the healer and guide.

He wanted me to be a healer, she thought. *And now I'm stuck with Charlie? Grandfather, are you sure this is the way it's supposed to be?*

She turned to Charlie. "Are you OK?"

"Yes, why?"

"You've gone through a lot in the last two days, and so have I."

"I know." he paused. "And I'm putting the pieces together, too.

I think Clara would be at the farm. Is there any reason we've traveled so long to be so far from the time we're searching for?

Tianna slouched her shoulder and let her neck glide down. She smiled and sighed. "I'm tired. Why can't we go to that nice village over there, by the lake? I think it's Port Austin."

Charlie was puzzled. "Are you kidding me?"

"No. Not yet." As he turned, expecting a kiss, they slid into the bushes in front of the farmhouse. "Well, we're here." she finished.

They walked to the graveyard where Tianna bent down and touched Clara's earth. "She's here." They bumped backward, day by day, until Clara was not in her grave.

"Looks like lost data again."

"Yup, let's see what the story is," she said.

It was July in 1871. It had been hot all spring and Clara was working in the kitchen. Arnold walked up to her. "Your brother Bill will find God and sober up. He just has a troubled mind."

Clara smiled. "I know. He was always the creative one, and crazy."

Anna, Clara's young granddaughter and Jimmy's wife, ran into the room and asked. "Grandma, why did you have children? If you didn't have my mother, I wouldn't be suffering in this life."

Grandma didn't respond. Ever since the loss of her babies, the poor girl was a little off. Clara tried to talk to her, and her husband Arnold tried. He just got a slap on the face.

Charlie was ready to ask if they should bump back when Clara gasped for air, grasped her chest, her eyes filled with fear, muscles clenching, teeth grinding, and her mind passing from the realm.

Tianna's first instinct was to rush to her. On her knees, she turned to Charlie and said, "Imagine Anna's state of mind after this." They watched as Anna found her grandmother on the floor. She cried and hugged her like a baby wanting mother.

Arnold helped Clara's brother Bill put Clara's body in the parlor to get ready for the funeral. Bill's best friend, Clarence, from Caseville, arrived early in the morning for the funeral. The two men went outside to talk and drink.

Tianna smiled, "Look at how many friends and family loved this special woman."

Charlie laughed. "Hey, I think she's a witch or something. She's the Bad Axe Woman ghost who is always around Farmer Bill. Clarence follows the two of them like a puppy."

"You put it so eloquently." She said wryly, "Sometimes you

men can be so brash."

They studied the timeline; again, the burial data was missing. "This is getting old," Charlie said. "Are we ready to see Farmer Bill die?"

"Not really." Tianna jotted several notes into her cell phone. "We can move forward, but slowly. The time we are going through culminates in the fire of 1871."

"Yes, Tianna, I know the story. Harry said he remembered Farmer Bill burning to death. I bet he dies in this fire. That would be October 8, 1871. Right?" he asked as he hopped on his Sea-Doo.

Tianna agreed with Charlie and headed for the period just before the fire. As they passed through the summer and early fall, they saw a parched landscape. The lumbering of Huron County's woods left mountains of dried branches. Farmers toiled at clearing the land for agriculture. Every fallen tree had a stump and roots that had to be pulled. Many of them were lined up around the field.

Scattered fires filled the air with acrid smoke, making it difficult to breathe. Tianna calculated the date, stopped, and touched the ground.

She walked back to Charlie and said, "He's not there, but we are close. They bumped ahead by two days and watched the sky turn dark with smoke. Day became night. Then a sudden burst of flames crossed the fields.

Charlie had the urge to run while Tianna was calm. She bumped forward, a day at a time. "The farmhouse didn't get destroyed during this fire," she advised, "and Bill is in the grave."

Charlie studied the days prior and after the fire of 1881. "I didn't see Farmer Bill or his friend Clarence around the farm. How are we going to find him?"

"Let's go back to the burial of Clara. If we watch the days or weeks after her death, perhaps we will discover where Bill and Clarence went." Tianna suggested.

The week after Clara's burial, Clarence and Arnold had an argument. Arnold accused him of corrupting Bill and turning him toward evil. Clarence looked like he was about to strike the larger Arnold, but Bill walked in and stopped him.

Bill turned to Arnold and said, "I know you can't understand my feelings for Clarence, but I love him. It may be a sin, but it's my sin, not Clarence's. We are moving out tomorrow."

"And where do you plan on living? You know, no one wants the two of you around. You are an abomination in our way of life. A vile, shameful curse."

Later that day, Bill and Clarence loaded their belongings onto a small wagon. Arnold was standing next to the wagon as Bill adjusted the reins on the horse.

"Bill, the words I spoke this morning were in anger. I loved your sister, and she loved me. You will always be a part of my family, and I am sorry. Please forgive me and know that you are always welcome here. Especially for our Sunday services."

Bill's head hung low, turned to Clarence, and he smiled. "Arnold, thank you. I will be back for your service on Sunday. We are going to work on the Blackburn farm, across the way. They have room in a barn that we can share."

Charlie and Tianna followed the wagon for a few hours and watched them settle into their new home. The two men worked in the fields, harvesting some crops, clearing fields of rubble, and enjoying each other.

Charlie commented, "Have you noticed how neither of them are getting drunk, like they were before Clara's death?"

"Yes, perhaps they found peace."

The day of the fire, Bill was in a field piling branches. There were several small fires burning, as everyone was taking advantage of the hot weather. That morning, fire raced across the

Midwest. Chicago was burning, and a string of fires jumped across the land.

Bill tried to run, but he was overtaken by flames and lay burnt crisp in the field. The following day, Clarence found his partner, and fell on his knees, wept, and then rushed away. He soon returned with Arnold and the horse and wagon.

The two men bundled Bill's remains and loaded him into the back of the wagon: they slowly rode back to Arnold's farmhouse. The farm was spared as the fire jumped irrationally through the county.

The funeral was small, as many families were burying their dead and trying to reconcile their losses. At the funeral, Arnold spoke about the importance of family. "You are all my children and through you my life is richer. As we lose our friends and family, we are reminded how fragile our lives are. Bill was family and a friend to many. Though he was not pure in soul, his heart was big and joyful. He will always be with us."

Charlie laughed when he heard the last sentence of Arnold's eulogy. *He will always be with us.*

"Tianna, is Arnold a good guy or a bad guy?"

Tianna thought for a moment. "I don't know. Sometimes he's prophetic, but I don't see him as demonic."

More fucking big words, Charlie thought to himself.

Tianna heard him but didn't comment.

She bumped through the future and stopped at the farm a few months later. It was January, and there was a light snow on the graveyard. She touched the earth and said, "Clarence is here."

"Let's go back to the farm where he and Bill were living," Charlie suggested. When they reached the farm, there was only rubble where the barn once stood. The barn was gone, and there was no sign of Clarence.

Let's go back and follow Clarence. We know he was at the

funeral, so that is where we should start. He must have moved somewhere.

They found Clarence living in an old log cabin on Arnold's farm. Tianna and Charlie watched the man drink himself into a stupor every night. Arnold tried several times to console him, but Clarence was on a self-destruction course. The man he loved was now dead, and he saw no future for himself. Of course, alcohol only made him more depressed.

That final day in January, Clarence grabbed a rope and walked into the woods. He tied the rope around a branch, climbed up, and jumped with the rope around his neck.

Charlie didn't want to watch, because he knew what the Caseville Man carried under his arm. Clarence fell to the ground, and his head landed next to him. Tianna cringed and looked like she was getting sick.

"Are you OK?" Charlie asked.

"Yes, I will be," she replied.

The funeral was held in Arnold's parlor. Charlie was not shown. He was in a covered pine box. Again there was no record of the burial.

CHAPTER 37

Charlie suggested going back to Harry's farmhouse, but Tianna was eager to move forward. "We have three more deaths to study," she said.

"No. We have ten more deaths to study," suggested Charlie. "There are sixteen graves, and we have completed six."

Tianna laughed, "So you can actually do addition?"

Charlie didn't find her question helpful, *but she is the boss,* he thought.

Tianna checked her phone notes and said, "The next person to die is Jimmy, then Orville, and Anna. The only person we haven't already met is Orville.

The two teens began their search for the timeline of Jimmy's death at the graveyard. Once they found him in the grave, they moved back in time, searching for him. They found him at the farm where he and his estranged wife, Anna, were living with Arnold. Orville was also there. Orville was a large man in his fifties.

After the devastating fire of 1871, many people were left homeless. Arnold's home was spared and having a need for people around him, he opened his home and heart for many. Tianna and Charlie watched the menagerie of people passing through the house and small sheds on Arnold's property. Charlie wondered how many of these people would be in the graveyard when they were finished.

Jimmy's grave was occupied in April 1883. There was no record of his burial, and Tianna found him in the woods. It was a beautiful warm Sunday in April, and Jimmy and Angela, a forty-some year-old woman, were engaged in intercourse under a tree next to the creek. Jimmy's wife turned off all sex with him, so he had a lot of pent up energy. Angela was in a similar situation.

There was a rustle. Charlie looked up and saw a man aim his rifle and shoot. Jimmy flopped like a stuck pig, and the woman screamed and ran toward the house. The gunman approached poor Jimmy and put him out of his misery by stomping his heavy boot into his head.

Two men rushed him and wrestled the gun from his hands. They carried Jimmy's body to the house and walked the killer into the barn where he was tied up.

When Jimmy's wife, Anna, saw her husband's bloody body, she laughed. The maniacal laugh of someone out of their mind. Arnold led her out of the room and asked her to stay in her corner.

The county sheriff was summoned, and the killer taken away. Tianna and Charlie wondered what the trial was like, but that wasn't part of their mission.

The funeral was attended by all who lived with Arnold and Jimmy's mother and older sister.

Tianna and Charlie moved forward to find Orville's death. Tianna estimated that he died shortly after Jimmy. It was early May, and Orville was in a field across from the farmhouse. He was behind a huge horse, rigged with a harness and ready to pull a plow. The shiny steel plow was a new addition to Arnold's farm. It replaced a smaller plow, which was difficult to use.

Orville was ready to plow when the bellyband slipped. He walked up to the horse and said, "Whoa there, boy." Pulling the strap tighter, Orville slipped and fell under the horse. As he pulled himself up, the horse bolted and the steel plow ran through his leg. He became tangled in the harness lines and was pulled along as the horse ran. When the horse stopped, it was in front of Arnold's home and Orville's limp, bloody, and dead body lay on the ground.

The funeral became a celebration of life. Even though Orville and Jimmy were now departed, life seemed better. Arnold invited friends and family to a feast and religious event. He praised his friends, praised God, asked God to care for the souls of his dead friends, and suggested, "We are all family. My family."

Again, the burial data was missing. "You know," Charlie commented, "we really need to figure out why the burials aren't visible."

"I know. For now, I want to concentrate on the deaths. I have a feeling we may find the reason for the missing data along the way."

The two teens slipped into the time stream to bump ahead. They watched as Anna became more unhinged. She seldom left the house. Arnold forced her to be a cook in exchange for her room and board, but it was obvious to Tianna and Charlie that she was becoming insane. Tianna put it best. "You can see it in her eyes. A madness... a sickness that won't let her rest."

Tianna considered her death a blessing. She lay in her corner, a blanket pulled around her head, resting on a pillowcase stuffed with some clothing.

Arnold entered the room and yelled at her to get breakfast ready. There was no answer to his demand. He walked up to the fragile woman and shook her. Those crazed eyes were open and staring at him, without life behind them. She was dead.

***

Both Tianna and Charlie were exhausted. Watching these deaths was a trying ordeal.

After a long pause, Tianna spoke. "I want out of the

realm."

They both opened their eyes as they sat in the bedroom silently. Charlie said, "Your wish has been granted. Do you want to tell the team what we learned, or could we just rest for a while?"

Carol opened the door and peaked in. "You're back?"

"Yes, Grandma Carol. Tianna wants to rest, and I would like to go to the mobile home and take a long hot shower." He looked at his watch and was surprised that only five hours had passed.

Carol stepped into the room and sat in the chair next to the bed. "We're preparing dinner now. Lila and Jonathon are making a beef roast with potatoes, gravy, salad, and cherry pie. You two have about two hours to rest.

Charlie jumped up and opened the door. "Tianna, I'll see you for dinner."

She smiled and said, "Only if I wake up."

She proceeded to lay down, pull a pillow under her head and closed her eyes.

Carol walked into the living room where Harry and Roger were having drinks and talking.

Roger was first to speak. "Well?"

Harry added, "Yes. Well?"

Carol questioned, "Well, what?"

They laughed and Carol announced, "I need a Bloody Mary. I have no idea what the kids found in their search, however; I will tell you that the process must be excruciating. They came back looking like they walked through the Sahara."

"I can imagine. Almost like Post Stress Syndrome," Roger suggested. "The stress of seeing all those lives at the time of their deaths, must take a toll."

"I understand, Roger," Harry approached. "I have lived it and through it. Let Tianna and Charlie rest, and we can talk when they are ready."

"Very good, gentlemen," Carol added with her drink in hand.

***

Lila and Jonathon argued in the kitchen. A circle of flesh dancing around the kitchen ended in a long kiss.

"I told you the temperature should be balanced to the size of the roast; given the time we have to cook."

"You know, you're sexy when you lecture me."

"Piss off and start the potatoes."

"Yes, dear. Potatoes are the plan."

"Where are the potato buds?"

"Under the sink in a bag."

"Damn, no instant?"

"No."

"How much time do we have?"

"I'm not sure. Let me check."

"Half an hour or less, I guess."

***

Charlie and Tianna reunited just before Lila announced that dinner was served. It was a rather formal family dinner. Chairs around the table and everyone assigned a seat. Of course, Carol, with Roger at her side, sat at one end and Harry at the other. Lila and Jonathon survived, and Tianna and Charlie faced them.

The dishes passed faster than the conversation. It was apparent the conversation needed some lubricating, so Charlie said, "We discovered that Farmer Bill and Clarence were lovers."

Conversations stopped. Harry broke out laughing and slapped Roger's back. "See, I told you I have some really queer ghosts."

Conversations returned to their former level. Tianna nudged Charlie's leg. "I hope you weren't making fun of Bill and Clarence."

"No, don't be silly. I just wanted to break the ice in this room. Do you want to tell everyone what we found?"

Tianna looked puzzled. "What did we find?"

Charlie couldn't answer the question.

The dinner conversation covered the fact that there were only two sets of bones left to surface in the graveyard. They were Robert and Arnold. Charlie and Tianna updated everyone on which people they watched die and the circumstances of their lives.

Everyone complimented Lila and Jonathon on the great dinner, but no one offered to help clean the kitchen. Carol was dragged out of a conversation with Roger to help. She didn't appreciate the intrusion, but she obliged.

Mid evening, Lila and Jonathon made their exit. Charlie cautioned Lila, "You better not be rocking the mobile home when I get there. I'm looking for a good night's sleep. Tianna and I have a difficult day ahead."

Lila laughed, "I'll try to be done by the time you return."

Before separating, Tianna and Charlie talked about today, tomorrow, and the future. They both agreed that it was worth the effort, and this time they might be able to have a relationship, other than a brother's friend, an older jazzman, or a hero of her people.

Charlie walked through the yard to the mobile home. Before reaching his destination, Cora ran up to him and tried to grab his hand. He studied the large hole in the back of her head, and the small hole in her forehead. But the look in her eyes was almost... gleeful.

"What do you want, young girl, another chance to feel

Charlie up?" When he heard his words, he cringed. "Damn, that's crass."

She smiled broadly, and Charlie responded, "Sorry, girl, not tonight; I have a headache."

She disappeared in a mist and Charlie continued to bed. He noticed Jonathon was freed from Lila's web and sleeping on the couch.

Charlie's night was filled with dreams from the day and the three-hundred-some years he has lived. There were several episodes with him and Tianna, entangled with ghosts, snakes, and reptiles. A dark cloud brewed above them and lightning flashed as a crescendo of sound engulfed them.

He could feel the ghosts surrounding him. When he opened his eyes, he was on the grass with sixteen ghosts encircling him, looking down, making him feel ever so small.

How did I get here? he asked himself. *Am I dreaming?*

Farmer Bill answered, "Only if we are also dreaming."

Charlie didn't know how to respond. He couldn't tell if he was or wasn't awake. Tianna walked into the circle, separating the ghosts. She offered Charlie her hand, and he stood facing her. He asked, "Am I sleeping, yet?"

Tianna smiled and replied, "Sort of. I think the ghosts want to communicate with us. This is the oddest thing I've seen so far. Ghosts that protect each other and their remains and communicate through our dreams."

The Bad Axe Woman stepped into the circle. "You two have to leave. I know you have been watching our past life. You are intruding on our world. If you continue, you will destroy everything."

Tianna calmly replied, "We're only here to help you find the peace, love, and joy of your own family."

Farmer Bill injected, "This is our family."

A bolt of lightning filled the sky with light. The connection was broken, and Charlie and Tianna woke in their separate beds.

Charlie tried to send a message. *Are you OK?*

Yes, see you in the morning. Tianna replied.

Charlie wished Tianna was in the room with him. He imagined that his hand was hers and quickly found relief.

CHAPTER 38

The rains started in the middle of the night. Charlie stood in the doorway watching the ghosts mill around in the woods. Cora and Roger faced Arnold as he talked; Farmer Bill and Clarence talked together next to the farmhouse, and the Bad Axe Woman comforted Casandra and Anna.

Jonathon exited the bathroom, toweling off as he walked to his couch. "If you hurry, you can get a shower before Lila wakes."

Lila's voice rang out, "Like hell, you can." The bathroom door slammed shut.

Charlie sat at the counter in his boxer briefs, sipping instant coffee while checking his email and messages. He messaged his friend Liz all about Tianna, and she told him about a new friend she'd made.

He turned toward Jonathon and asked, "Tell me, John Boy, why do you let that woman play you? Does she even love you?"

Jonathon laughed. "I sure as hell hope she doesn't. That would complicate our relationship." He pulled his jeans up and buckled his belt. "There is nothing better than having a regular sex partner with no strings attached. I know she can be a bitch, but so can I."

Charlie smiled at the idea. "OK, but I think she's a bigger bitch than you are."

Lila, now standing behind Charlie, said. "You better not be calling me a bitch, Twerp."

"Not me," Charlie laughed. "I was commenting on something John Boy said. Don't worry, Lila. Some of us like bitches."

"Piss off." She turned toward the bedroom. "You can use the bathroom, now. Oh, I think the hot water is gone."

***

Carol and Tianna sat at the kitchen table talking about Charlie, Harry, Roger, and the Ghosts.

Tianna asked, "Will you be able to exhume the last graves in this rain?"

"Not until it stops and dries off. The meteorologist says that might happen early afternoon. If we get Robert's bones dug out today, that would be major. Are you up to seeing more deaths?"

"I have to be."

"You and Charlie looked exhausted when you returned yesterday."

"I know. It didn't help that we're also building our relationship."

"Is there one?" Carol sipped her hot coffee and added, "Be careful Tianna, Charlie isn't really mature yet, and I don't want my grandson to get hurt."

"In reality, Charlie's soul is older than mine by over 75 years." She reached for a slice of buttered toast, took the Michigan cherry jam, and piled it high. "His memories are returning and he's maturing quickly."

Carol nodded. "How are you doing?"

"I'm fine. I have a few issues to iron out, though."

"Such as?"

"I am engaged to get married, and now I am rethinking that plan. Again."

"Wow. When did this happen and who is the lucky man?"

"My high school boyfriend, Eddie. He asked me before school started. The problem is, he's going to college in Detroit, I'm in Ann Arbor, and now I'm falling in love with your grandson."

"Welcome to womanhood, my dear. We are always facing decisions."

They laughed. Tianna enjoyed her jam-topped toast and then said, "Carol, I think I accepted Eddie's proposal because he is a safe choice. Every time I fell in love, head over heels, I got myself killed by the Guardians. The feelings I have for Charlie are like those I had in my previous lives." She thought carefully. "Do I want to take that chance?"

"I can't tell you what to do, but don't hurt my grandson or you'll have to deal with me as well as those Guardians."

***

After breakfast, Carol shut the bedroom door. Charlie and Tianna sat facing each other, holding hands on the bed.

Tianna asked, "Are you ready to witness more deaths?"

"No, but the job has to be done. These ghosts are getting under my skin, and into my mind."

"Gotcha."

In an instant, the two were standing next to the farmhouse facing the graveyard. Tianna walked over to Omar's grave. "Nope, not here yet."

They moved ahead until the body was in the ground.

Charlie suggested, "Why don't we walk it back a week and look at what's happening in Arnold's world. Perhaps we will learn who this Omar is."

As the two teens watched the farm, they noticed many people working and living with Arnold. Omar was a twenty-year-old man. Arnold gave him a job clearing the woods of rubble and trees still standing after the fire of 1871.

Charlie and Tianna studied each person in the house. There were also several men living in the small barn, and an Indian named Chester was living in a hut behind the graveyard.

There were now small wooden markers with hand carved names for each grave. Charlie watched Tianna walk around the grave markers. She made notes and said, "Today is March 15, 1875. I think we should follow Omar." She pointed to the young man, dressed in warm layers of clothing carrying an axe. He was followed by Chester and Robert. They carried a large two-man saw.

The three men walked about a quarter mile and entered a field filled with many tree stumps and piles of branches. Today their mission was to fell the last three trees standing in the field.

Omar yelled, "Let's get these trees cut down, boys."

Chester cussed, "Who you calling boys, boy."

"Get over it, Chester."

Robert laughed and grabbed one end of the two-saw. Chester took the other end, and like a well-tuned machine, they slid the teeth back and forth through the tree trunk. Robert stopped halfway through, and Omar took his axe and cut a wedge where he wanted the tree to fall.

Once done, the boys continued with the saw as Omar walked toward the next tree. Chester and Robert didn't notice Omar returning. They continued to saw. The tree cracked and fell toward Omar.

Robert yelled, "Get out of the way, Omar." It was too late. The tree crushed the young man, killing him.

Chester took off running toward the farm. He turned back and yelled, "I'll get Arnold. He can help us get the tree off Robert."

Arnold helped clear the tree, and Chester and Robert pulled Omar's lifeless body from under its weight. The somber men carried Omar back to the farmhouse, where they layed him out, in the parlor for viewing. The funeral was two days later, and over twenty individuals attended it.

Arnold gave another long sermon, and then he invited everyone to enjoy the feast the women had prepared. Charlie reminded Tianna that Chester, a child named Allan, and a woman named Angela were the next deaths to review.

"Yes, I am aware of that," she replied.

During the funeral, Tianna and Charlie studied all the mourners and identified Allan. He was the son of Mary Beth, a housekeeper and cook who lost her husband in the 1871 fire. Mary Beth didn't have a family or a home to go to, so Arnold offered her a place to live in exchange for her services. He loved that he had the five-year-old boy around the house.

"Let's bump ahead," suggested Tianna. As they moved through the months, they watched how Arnold kept welcoming more strangers into his home. Every Sunday more people attended Arnold's worship service.

"Have you noticed how Arnold spends more time preaching about his family than about God and Jesus?" Tianna asked.

"Yes. I think it's an ego thing for Arnold. He's the type of person who has to have people around him. I bet he lived a very lonely childhood."

Thanksgiving was approaching, and Mary Beth was busy preparing pies and bread. The harvest was good, and the root cellar was filled with vegetables, crocks of sauerkraut, and smoked and salted meats. Thanksgiving this year would feature fresh roast venison.

Charlie and Tianna noticed that Mary Beth's son was looking pale and appeared to be losing weight. "I wonder if he's sick," Tianna asked as the boy walked into the kitchen, crying.

Arnold suggested Robert ride into Bad Axe and fetch the new doctor. After being gone for a few hours, a horse and small buggy pulled into the yard. A tall slender man, carrying a black case and dressed in a suit, entered the farmhouse.

"Where is the boy?" he asked.

Mary Beth led him to the parlor where the youngster was sleeping on a makeshift bed.

The doctor examined the boy and gave Mary Beth some medicine. "I'm not sure what is causing your son's anemia, but give him this, twice a day. If he isn't better in a few days, bring him to my office next week."

Three days before Thanksgiving, they found Allan dead. He passed in his sleep with his weeping mother holding the boy in her arms. Arnold cried, which surprised Charlie. Tianna suggested, "It's always hard to accept the death of a child," but Charlie thought... *there must be more to it.*

At the funeral Arnold confessed he wanted to adopt Allan as his own son. The son he never had.

The funeral was the day before Thanksgiving of 1875, and despite the death of Allan, everyone said they were thankful.

***

Tianna and Charlie moved forward in search of Chester and Anna's deaths. It was a tranquil time between 1875 and 1880. The farm grew; Arnold sold land and conducted business in Bad Axe, Sebewaing, Port Austin, and Sand Beach.

Charlie suggested following Arnold when he announced that he and Chester would ride the train to Detroit.

"What do you hope to discover?" Tianna asked.

"I'm not sure, but we must have missed something. Watching everyone die isn't helping us discover the secret of the ghosts, is it? Perhaps we should learn more about this man. Where does his money come from? Why is he so intent on having people around him, and why does he act like a preacher?"

The trip revealed that Arnold's family was very wealthy. His father, a banker and businessman, purchased several thousand acres in the Bad Axe area for his son, so he could avoid being drafted into the Civil War. On this trip, Arnold met with his family and old friends.

Tianna and Charlie learned Arnold was the only son, and his father was elderly. Since Arnold did not have a son, the family business would go to his sister's son. This upset Arnold, and he left the meeting abruptly.

Tianna and Charlie agreed they learned nothing to indicate why the ghosts were trapped in the graveyard, so they searched for Chester and Angela's deaths.

It was a few days before Christmas of 1880. Arnold gave Angela money and asked her to go with Chester to Bad Axe, where there was a general store. "I want you to buy gifts for everyone."

She questioned what to buy, and he suggested clothing, bedding, and something special for each of his guests. He gave her more money than she had ever seen. He then said, "Take these twenty dollars and spend it on yourself." She was overwhelmed with gratitude.

It was a bitter December day, so she grabbed a blanket and climbed aboard the buckboard wagon. Chester had loaded several bags of flour that Arnold wanted him to deliver to the general store. It should have been a quick ride, but the path was filled with ruts from the recent thaw and refreeze, and snow stood at least a foot deep with drifts over two feet.

As they slowly progressed, Angela noticed Chester looked pallid. "Are you OK?" she asked. He didn't answer. She tapped his shoulder, and he fell forward, off and under the wagon. She screamed, grabbed the reins, and halted the horse.

Chester was dead. Being a small woman, Angela used every ounce of her strength and pulled Chester onto the back of the

A Killer Within

wagon. She found a place to turn the wagon around and returned to the farm. Arnold saw the wagon and rushed to assist her. They took Arnold into the parlor and laid him on the table.

One woman helped Angela out of her wet clothes and prepared Chester for viewing. Death was a hands-on process.

The funeral took place on Christmas Eve, and Arnold's Christmas sermon was more about death and dying than the birth of Christ. Angela couldn't be at the funeral or Christmas celebration; she was in bed with chills. The doctor visited, but within days, she was dead. The doctor said it was pneumonia.

Arnold was emotional during her funeral, and all the guests knew he loved her.

Within minutes of the funeral, Charlie and Tianna opened their eyes. Tianna broke into tears, and Charlie reached across and hugged her. He wished he could ease her sorrow, but he didn't know how.

Carol heard the two teens and entered the bedroom. She saw the state Tianna was in and helped her out of the room. She took her aside, and the two talked for over an hour. Charlie asked Roger for help with his sorrow. Something he never expected to do.

CHAPTER 39

Carol and Roger would not allow Tianna and Charlie to return to the realm again today. Tianna wanted to finish the task, but Roger said, "No! You can finish tomorrow morning."

Carol added, "The two of you need to relax and talk. I know you are both strong, but you have witnessed thirteen deaths in two days. My God, look at yourselves. You're both ready to crack. Talk about what you've seen and let us help. I know you feel you haven't learned enough about the ghosts, but perhaps if you tell us what you've seen, we can help fill in the details."

Charlie walked over to Carol and put his arm around her and said, "We will tell you the entire story we've witnessed. Just give us some time to gather ourselves. It is true," he turned to Tianna, "watching people die is not a simple task."

Roger smiled and asked, "Harry, what are we going to do for dinner around here tonight?"

Harry said, "I'm hungry for Chinese takeout. Anyone else?"

Everyone agreed that a feast from China King would be ideal. Harry suggested, "Why don't the two of you relax; get comfortable. We won't be eating for a few hours, so if you want, I have some old movies, or we can play a board game or cards."

Charlie laughed. "I guess that is the generation gap, isn't it, Tianna?"

"Yes, I think so. I'm going to freshen up. You old guys can watch your old movies while we play on our phones and chill."

184

Tianna and Charlie hugged. He initiated, "I'll be outside in fifteen minutes. If you like we can have some tea."

She bowed slightly and said, "At your pleasure, sir." Then she waltzed out of the room.

***

Standing under the hot shower, Charlie watched his past lives flash before himself. He looked back in time and then forward... imagining where his life would lead.

Tianna dropped her towel and stepped under her flowing shower. Her favorite lotion soothed her mocha skin, and she smiled at the thought of Charlie standing in the tiny mobile home shower. *You should be over here; I think we have more water on this side of the ocean,* she thought.

Fifteen minutes later, Charlie stood next to the graves. *Jonathon has been very productive with that small backhoe,* he thought.

They now filled almost all the graves with dirt, packed down with the sod replaced. He noticed how much the graveyard looked like the original. *Leave it to those fucking FBI guys to have all their tracks covered. The FBI wouldn't dare let people know there are ghosts south of Bad Axe.*

Harry approached Charlie. "That looked like an interesting thought. Hope it's nothing bad."

"No, Harry." Charlie recalled. "Just a random thought. You seem to handle the situation with ease."

"As well as can be expected. I hope you and Tianna have some information to share."

Charlie thought for a moment. "The problem we have is that you are the only one with a memory of the burials."

"And that is important," Tianna added as she approached.

Harry watched the group of ghosts at the edge of the woods

and said loudly, "I would hate to see things get eviler around here. I think we've had enough already." Harry projected his voice across the graveyard and into the woods. "I'm afraid my ghosts are getting restless."

Roger and Carol approached, and Lila and Jonathon circled the group.

Tianna broke out laughing. "Now tell me again, who are the ghosts around here? Them or us?"

Charlie smiled. "I think they are," he pointed toward the woods, "but the way things are going, it's anyone's guess."

Carol asked, "I thought you were going to rest."

"That was the plan," responded Tianna. "But it might be smart to go over what we know."

Roger suggested sitting at the patio table. He grabbed his notebook and sat down. Harry grabbed a beer, and within minutes of a mad dash, everyone's eyes were on Tianna.

She sat down next to Charlie and took his hand. "Are we ready for this?" she asked.

"Yes, I think so."

She cleared her throat. "As we told you before, Harry has the only memory of the burials. The data in the realm for these events has been mysteriously removed. I have been in communication with the Guardians of the realm, and they will be with us tomorrow while we finish our investigation."

"What can they do to protect the timeline?" Carol asked.

Tianna looked to Charlie. "Any ideas?"

"Well, if my memory serves me correctly, they are the official keepers of all time past. If anyone can solve a problem in this realm, they can."

Tianna chuckled, "I hope."

The teens described each person buried in the graveyard and summarized how they died. With all the questions asked, Charlie checked the time. It took well over two hours.

Harry said, "Your description of these people leaves me speechless."

"Why?" asked Tianna.

"Because it's as if I were there. I know them better than my family, and it scares me. It scares the hell out of me. It makes me question who I am. What I am." Harry stood, turned, and put his hands on the counter.

Carol and Roger put their arms around their friend. Carol spoke. "You are the kind man who cared. They took your life, and yet you returned love."

Charlie was blunter. "Harry, I think these ghosts screwed you."

Tianna pleaded, "Harry! We don't know what happened. But trust me, you are a strong and good man and have nothing to fear."

Harry turned and laughed. "Lila and Jonathon, what's your opinion?"

Jonathon stood. "Harry, I agree with Charlie. It kills me to say that, but the Indian dude speaks true. Those ghosts fucked you."

Harry burst into laughter, an enormous smile on his face. "God, I am so lucky to have met you guys. My new family."

Carol kissed him, and Roger patted his ass. Jonathon noticed and smiled.

Lila stood and said, "Hey! What about my opinion?"

The room grew quiet. Carol said, "I'm sorry Lila. It was rude of me. What do you think?"

Lila's face grew serious. She thought for a moment. "Guys, enough with the fucking ghost joke." She looked at Tianna and continued, "The space between our time, here and now, and that of the family you observed from the past, is very small. In the billions of years in all of time, it is less than an electron. But sometimes our paths (like electrons) cross, intertwine, and collide. I think what happened to Harry resulted from a terrible mistake in time. Somehow he was sensitive and saw the ghosts, and he suffered because he couldn't share his fears."

"Wow." Tianna smiled. "I just hope when we find what mistake occurred, we can put everything back together."

***

Tianna and Charlie had time to sit quietly in the living room while the kitchen was cleared.

Tianna struggled for words and then said, "I have to tell you something."

Charlie straightened his back. "Sounds serious. Are you going to tell me I was once your first cousin?"

"No, silly. It's more serious than that. I am engaged to get married." She hesitated and added, "well, I sort of am engaged... sort of."

Charlie's jaw dropped. "Surprise."

"Not to me. I'm bringing it up because I'm NOT sure I am committed to ever getting married."

"It sounds like a long story. We'll have to talk about it sometime. Does this change how we interact?" He slid closer and kissed her lips.

She kissed him back and said, "No. In fact you might make it easier for me to decide."

They hugged and then checked their phones for messages.

***

After a peaceful night, Tianna and Charlie were ready to stream into the timeline. They sat holding hands as the team stood outside the open door, watching.

Tianna looked at them and smiled. She wanted to wave but

thought *that would be silly.* Then she noticed Charlie winking at Carol and she saw the twinkle in her eye.

Carol shut the door and let the teens be.

"And away we go, into the wild blue yonder."

Tianna chuckled. "It's just a stream away,"

"I'm streaming of a white Christmas." Charlie sang.

They both laughed and slid toward the farmhouse in the woods. Tianna checked her phone. "It's late May 1881."

"The great fire is coming, so this could get hot." Charlie followed her as they walked around the house.

Tianna checked the backyard and said, "Perhaps it will be hotter than Hell."

Charlie thought for a moment. "That could be it. That great fire from Hell, sweeping over the land."

"It could be that simple." She touched the earth, and neither Cora nor Robert was there. "Want to look around or jump to Cora's death?"

"Let's see who Arnold is entertaining, first."

"You lead," she insisted.

Charlie was not shy; he marched into the farmhouse looking for people to suspect or respect. Sometimes it was hard to tell them apart.

After viewing the home, they met in the backyard next to a tree. Tianna was watching some chickens pecking for seeds, and in another corner, young girls, boys, and fathers and mothers, were working for and with Arnold.

Tianna commented, "He sure is a businessman, isn't he?"

"Yes." She pulled him along into the future. "So, Robert and Cora are lovers, and friends?" he mused.

"Oops, that doesn't look right." Tianna stopped, and they watched as Arnold and Cora exchanged in more than a comment. "How old is she, any guess?"

Charlie thought, "My guess, she's our age or older."

"I thought much younger. Well, I guess we're not here to judge, just discover."

Charlie laughed. "No, but we will judge, won't we?"

Robert suspected his girlfriend was cheating. On the first day of June 1871, Charlie and Tianna watched as Robert caught Cora and Arnold copulating in the parlor, like two wild animals. When Robert burst into the room, Arnold just grabbed his pants and walked away without a word. He let Cora handle her man; *she knows what to do to keep him smiling.*

"Damn it, Cora, why are you doing this. Is it his money? Oh God, does he pay you?"

"Jesus, no. Robert. He's given us stuff, but no money."

He grabbed a pile of paper from the table and threw them at her. Cora responded with, "Mr. Arnold will not be happy with you, and I'm going to be the mother of his child, a son we hope."

"The hell you are." Robert took a swing, his hand smashing across Cora's youthful face, knocking her down. "You will be dead before I let him plant his seed in you."

"Then you better wise up, because you are so dead. Arnold will take care of you. Go away little boy; I need a real man."

Robert picked up Arnold's revolver, pointed it to the center of Cora's forehead, and pulled the tiger.

His knees buckled, and he crashed down to his lover's level on the floor. Her dead eyes stared at him. He wept, pushed the barrel into his mouth, and pulled the trigger before Arnold could stop him.

Arnold was encircling the two slaughtered teenagers like an eagle, a tiger, or warlock protecting his family: his face calculating damages and liability.

Charlie took Tianna's hand. "That man is pure evil, isn't he?"

Two forms, wearing hooded, long, black gowns, flowing

to the ground, their faces blank and formless, appeared. *The Guardians, I assume.*

Energy reverberated, and the forms chimed, *Lovely to see you again, child. I see you have found a true warrior for your partner. Isn't time wonderful?*

"Charlie," Tianna introduced.

"Don't tell me, I know them. I remember meeting them before, many times."

He knew better than to offer a handshake or any warmth.

Tianna and Charlie walked back and forth with the two hooded guys. They wrote notes on their devices and hummed some strange songs.

Tianna looked at Charlie and smiled. She motioned her eyes, and he walked to her side for a private conversation.

Away from the Guardians, Charlie asked. "Are we good with them or do we have something to fear?"

Tianna watched the two as her lips said, "I want to have sex with you, and I sure hope we're good."

The taller Guardian spoke in a warm, low voice, "Don't worry. We aren't here to punish you, we are here as one, to be a part of you. Sir, it is a pleasure to meet you, again, and Tianna, keep that free spirit of yours alive and your request of Charlie may happen." The Guardians moved ahead in time, checked the memory loss, and stopped on a particularly hot October day.

Tianna said, "Do you feel that? The stillness, the depth of despair; is it a break in the timeline?"

Tall Guardian said, "No. This event did not break the time, it stretched it for many creatures when that ill wind blew through this area. It was a tragedy of biblical proportions. And ironically, it cleared the way for a growing community of merchants and farmers."

In every field, farmers were burning piles of branches and roots from the harvesting of the forest, forests now broken into smaller plots for farming.

"We're near, aren't we?" Charlie asked.

"Yes," the Guardians said in unison.

Tianna pointed to a wall of flames coming from the southeast. The sky grew dark with smoke, and the flames became a raging inferno.

Arnold yelled for his family to leave their belongings and get into the wagons. The animals were let loose so they could escape. Many of them ran toward the fire, but Arnold wasn't watching them. He helped the children into the wagon, hugged them, and yelled at the men to get going.

"What about you, Arnold?" one young boy yelled.

"I'll be fine, save yourselves. Go to Bad Axe. There should be a safe place there. Perhaps the county courthouse."

The wagons flew down the path and headed north as Arnold tried to clear around his house. *If I can keep the fire from my house, I will be safe,* he said aloud to himself.

The inferno came closer, and it was obvious that Arnold could not save his home. He ran to the backyard and gazed at the fifteen wooden markers in his graveyard. He fell to his knees to pray.

Charlie, Tianna, and the Guardians watched as the flames jumped to the dry grass, and then to Arnold's back. His clothing burst into flames, and a tornado of flames swirled around him.

Charlie cringed as he heard flesh sizzling and saw it turning black, like a photograph burning in the fireplace.

Tianna turned her head away, tears flowing down her cheeks. Arnold was dead, but still on his knees, as if in prayer.

A thunderous voice erupted from the flames. It was Arnold.

"God? Satan? One of you must let my family forever be with me."

The flames subsided, and his lifeless body collapsed to the ground.

Charlie hugged Tianna, and the two walked away. The Guardians poked at the ashes and moved forward in time. "We have a problem," said Tall Guardian.

Tianna nodded. "I know. Is this what trapped the ghosts and corrupted the timeline?"

Short Guardian spoke. "It's more complicated than that. Look." They moved forward in time. The sky was bright and a few people could be seen walking around in a daze. A young man walked into Arnold's backyard. There was nothing but the remains of the basement and the charred remains of Arnold.

The man walked to his wagon and brought back a shovel. He began digging a grave and rolled what was left of Arnold's body into it.

In surprise, Tianna said, "Charlie, the memory for this burial is here. But who is that man? He looks so familiar."

"He kind-of looks like Harry, but I don't think it's him."

Tall Guardian yelled, "We must return to the present, NOW!"

CHAPTER 40

Jonathon struggled with the backhoe while Lila and Carol finished Robert's grave. He yelled to Carol, "I don't know what is wrong with this machine, but it just has a mind of its own."

Lila laughed, "It's the operator."

Carol suggested, "Perhaps the ghosts have taken control. Forget the backhoe and use the shovel. You almost have the bones uncovered and the backhoe could damage them."

Jonathon jumped off the backhoe and picked up the shovel. He looked into the hole and saw what appeared to be light coming from under a stone at the bottom of the grave. "Hey, look at that. What's going on here?"

The hand of Tall Guardian touched his shoulder, and he almost fell into the grave, "What the hell?"

"Sorry, son. Please shovel a little more dirt into this grave."

Jonathon pushed dirt with his foot and covered the strange light. "And who the hell are you two?" His question went unanswered. The Guardians walked around, checking their notes and the timeline.

**

Carol saw Tianna and Charlie exit Harry's home. They ran to the gravesite and Tianna asked, "Is he still covered?" Within minutes, everyone was standing around Arnold's grave.

Roger asked, "So what happened that brought you back here?"

"We had to stop John Boy from uncovering the hornet's nest, that is Arnold." Charlie turned to watch the sixteen ghosts standing at the edge of the woods.

Tianna noticed and asked him, "Can you hear what they're saying?"

"No, but Clara is furious and I think she's ready to go to war."

Harry turned to the ghosts. "Stop it. Can't you see these wonderful people are trying to help you?"

Clara picked up a stick and raised it above her head. "Let's stop them. Don't let them destroy our home." The other ghosts picked up sticks and followed her lead, chanting, *kill them, kill them, kill...* They began circling the graveyard, making threatening motions.

Tall Guardian raised his hand, and everything went still. Like a frozen video, the ghosts stood with their weapons ready to strike. Time stopped for the ghosts, but the humans continued their work.

Harry asked Tall Guardian, "How long can you hold them back?"

"Long enough."

Charlie had to speak. "Harry, we saw someone bury Arnold. He looked like a younger you." He turned to Tianna and asked. "Didn't you say you've seen that person before?"

"Yes!" she screamed with delight and ran toward the farmhouse and returned with a small framed photograph.

Charlie asked, "Well, what is it?"

"Harry, this is the man who buried Arnold. Who is it?" She handed him the antique photograph. It was a tall man, built like Harry, with a slight beard and dark hair. Indeed, it looked like Harry.

Harry stood in silence.

Roger put his arm around his friend. "Well? Do you know

who it is?"

"Yes. It's my grandfather. He died when I was ten years old. He lived down the road and..." Tears filled Harry's eyes. "Oh my God. Grandpa."

Roger walked Harry to the patio table and sat him down. The team joined them.

Tall Guardian spoke. "Harry, your grandfather told you about the graves when you were a child, didn't he?"

"Yes."

"When did you see the first ghost?"

"The first night we lived in our new home. Grandpa said they were friendly and I shouldn't be afraid. But when he told me about each person who died here, I hurt so bad. I wanted to help them. I was afraid. I.... I.... I felt loved for the first time." Tears flowed as his memories changed before his eyes.

Short Guardian spoke, "You loved, and Arnold corrupted your love."

Tianna interrupted. "Harry, we can deal with your pain after we get your ghosts into their correct time."

"Yes," Charlie added. "Every minute is precious." He turned to Tianna and then the Guardians. "I assume you have the solution?"

"We do." The two hooded Guardians walked to the edge of Arnold's grave and knelt. Tall Guardian opened his hands, and a book appeared. It flew open and streamed images toward the sky. The words of God were being gathered and made ready to correct the past and let the souls of Arnold's family find their rightful place in the arms of their genuine families.

"Son," he said to Jonathon, "please unearth Arnold's bones, now."

Jonathon jumped into the grave and with his hands he uncovered the skull, arms, legs, feet... until all the bones were on the edge of the grave. Lila wanted to touch them, but Guardian wouldn't let her.

Tianna walked up with a glass of clear liquid. She handed it to Short Guardian. He mumbled words and hummed a quick tune. He then poured the liquid onto the bones, which sizzled, steam rising to the heavens. When they stopped, he said. "You can remove the bones, Lila."

Lila picked the bones up and placed them into her plastic container. She put the lid on and walked the bones into the lab.

Tall and Short Guardian stood and walked to the table where Harry sat. He was still thinking of the past and the recent memories of his grandfather, the memories of the burials, and the lovely people from the past who he knew all these years, living in the graveyard of his sorrow.

"We want you to watch what happens now," Tall Guardian said, as he helped Harry stand. They walked into the yard and faced the frozen ghosts who stood ready to kill them with their stick weapons, ready to save Arnold, their spiritual leader.

Charlie smiled and hugged Tianna. "Let the fun begin."

Short Guardian opened his arms and spoke in a thunderous voice. "You are free. You are One with God. Go forward without fear."

Arnold's ghost stood and crawled out of his grave. He looked around at his friends, both human and ghost. A broad smile graced his stern face, and he bellowed with laughter. He stepped toward the light where his father, mother, and sisters stood with open arms. He ran, stopped, and looked back. "Harry, I'm sorry. I didn't mean to hurt you. Please forgive me." With glee, he ran to his family and melted into the light.

The remaining fifteen ghosts morphed from an image of the living dead to the beings they were when alive, filled with hope and life.

Anne, dressed in a lovely lace dress, ran to her babies. Her husband at her side, the family waved back as they showed their parents and grandparents, their grandchildren. With hugs and kisses, they greeted their friends and then they walked into the light, never looking back.

Farmer Bill stood next to his lover, Orville. Bill's sister, the Bad Axe Woman, opened her arms and hugged the two men. They turned back and smiled. Bill spoke. "Harry, you have been a good friend, and we are sorry if we hurt you. Please forgive us." They thanked their ghost mates, turned toward the light, and walked into the arms of a huge extended family. The light flashed and they disappeared.

Harry grew in strength as his family found their place in time. He walked among them, shaking hands and hugging them as they prepared to move on. Tianna and Charlie watched with joy in their hearts as each ghost morphed into the light.

The last ghost to leave was Cora. She walked up to Tianna and said, "You're lucky. Charlie is so sexy; I wish he were mine. Oh well, you look like you can handle him."

Charlie smiled and gave her a hug. Her hand slid down and felt his ass. He grinned. "Vixen. Such a wicked woman." She grinned and walked toward Robert. Together, arm in arm, they disappeared into the light.

***

The Guardians approached Harry. Tall Guardian spoke, "The memories of the burials will fade by morning, and you will find comfort. Live your remaining years without fear; for you, like your ghosts, will have a wondrous future."

The Guardians turned and faded into a mist, blown away by the breeze.

Roger approached his friend and put his arm around him. "You know; God really loves you... doesn't he?"

Harry burst in laughter. Then tears, laughter and tears... as the weight of the past was, like the Guardians, dissolved into the air by the winds of truth. He caught his breath, touched Roger hand and smiled.

"The memories are fading, but new ones are taking their place. You were correct, my friend. God must really love me. He led me to you, and you showed me the past as it was, so now I can see my future in a new light. I didn't have to become a ghost to find the grace of God."

Roger stood back and looked at Harry. A stronger man, younger than he was on the first appointment. A man filled with life and love. The type of man he wished he could find for a partner. *No, he is a friend and patient. It is not the correct action for me to take.*

"Harry, you have lived a wonderful life. Your law firm stood for all that is good. I rarely say that about lawyers, but you were good. I mean a good man. That was why I just could not believe you were a killer."

"Thank you for believing in me. I am going to owe you big time, aren't I?"

Roger walked in a circle thinking and then said. "Yes. You are."

Jonathon was watching the two men and decided it appeared safe to approach.

"You two look like you're bonding nicely. Harry, I am glad you settled into your new reality. You look good. Roger, doesn't Harry look better than he did when we first met?"

Roger nodded and said, "Yes, he looks great. I think we three great looking men should go in and have many cold drinks?"

"That's what I'm talking about." Jonathon burst into laughter. "I'll get the cards. A three handed poker game is always a great way to celebrate the day."

Harry slapped Jonathon on the back, "You just want to take

our money?"

Jonathon didn't deny, but he wished for more.

***

A calmness fell over Harry's property. The woods filled with the songs of birds, and families of squirrels and rabbits took over spaces where the ghosts once dwelt.

Charlie and Tianna walked. Hand in hand, they strolled through the woods.

Tianna said, "I called Eddie. It must be kismet; he broke off our relationship. Something about finding his nerve to talk to other women. Now he's involved with a girl from Georgia. They're some classes together."

"And that means?"

"I am a free woman, Charlie. The Guardians said we could also be free and have a wondrous future. Isn't that glorious news?"

Charlie didn't answer. He bent down and picked up a dead branch.

"Well?" Tianna persisted.

"I'm thinking."

"About what?"

"About how we need to take it one step at a time."

"Charlie, I want to run. I've been taking small steps through-out my many lives and now I'm ready."

"I'm not sure I'm ready." Charlie turned his back to her. "I never could imagine myself saying this. Tianna, I love you." He turned and faced her. "I want to be with you forever. I just don't want our relationship to become a trap for either of us. Do you get what I'm saying?"

"Yes, and I need you to be like this. Sometimes I get over exuberant and don't think. You ground me and that's good. Can we take it to the next level?"

"If you're talking second base, yes."

"No. I'm talking about rounding third and heading for home."

"Tonight?" Charlie was hopeful.

"Tonight!" Tianna was positive.

They hugged and headed for home.

***

Carol and Lila were sitting in the living room. Soft music drifted from the stereo and a video played soundlessly on the television.

"Well," Lila sighed, "what happens now? Are you going to hook up with the old guy?"

"Don't talk like that, Lila. You know how much this means to us, to our family."

"Yes, dear. I know."

"I've always known," she repeated.

"This might be our last chance. So don't call me dear. You know I hate that. It's Carol." She relaxed. "Tell me, what is Charlie up to? He's changed so much, more like his grandfather every day. I knew he was special when I first saw him in the hospital. Kathy would be so proud of her grandson. I could never have dreamed he would become the young man he is today."

"Again, I ask," insisted Lila, "When are you going to tell him he's adopted, and not your daughter's son?"

"Quiet. I think Harry is coming into the room." She looked toward the doorway and saw that it was Charlie and Tianna.

"Are you two enjoying the fruits of your efforts? I know I am." She smiled and picked up her empty wine glass. "Charlie, why don't you get me and Lila another bottle of wine from the cooler. And bring glasses for you and Tianna."

Tianna and Charlie walked into the kitchen, where Roger, Harry, and Jonathon were in the middle of their poker game.

"From the looks of the chips, it's obvious John Boy is the big winner," Charlie declared.

"Yes, I am kid. If you want to lose some of the money your grandma's paying you, why don't you sit down with the boys and let me fleece you, too," Jonathon suggested.

"No." Charlie grabbed the wine as Tianna pulled two glasses from the cupboard. "Tianna and I are going to bring this wine to Grandma. We just want a nice, relaxing evening." He winked at Tianna.

After pouring wine into their glasses, Charlie and Tianna took their glasses and walked upstairs to her room. Both of them were nervous.

Tianna hesitantly said, "You know, in this lifetime I have only been with Eddie, and he's not the wild lover I think you might be."

"I understand. I haven't been past third base many times either, but I fantasize a lot."

"Fantasies can be fun, can't they?" An idea flashed across her mind.

Tianna set her glass on the end table next to Charlie's and reached for his hands. They sat on the bed, facing each other.

"I have an idea. Let's go into the realm and travel back to Detroit, during the thirties. I know this wonderful ballroom where we can dance and find a romantic spot to make love."

"OK. So, now we're going to make love in the realm?"

"Yes, virtual love, isn't that a hoot?"

With a strong breeze in their face, the two streamed through the timeline and landed in front of the Vanity Ballroom, on the corner of Newport and Jefferson. The hall had just opened and a steady line of customers walked through the double doors. Charlie studied the beautifully decorated building with an art deco... Aztec design with multicolor Mayan carvings. He smiled and said, "I remember this place. I think my jazz band played here. What year is it?"

Tianna checked her phone. "It's 1930. The ballroom opened in 1929 on the day the Wall Street stock market crashed.

"Come on, we don't need to wait in line." She walked through the crowd of well-dressed patrons. The entrance led to a grand staircase to the upstairs ballroom.

Charlie was awestruck. "I'm positive I've danced here before. It looks like an Aztec temple."

On the stage Duke Ellington and his band played *Mood Indigo*, a moody jazz number. Tianna rushed Charlie onto the maple dance floor and snuggled next to him as they danced under the huge revolving chandelier with light-reflecting mirrors.

Charlie couldn't keep his eyes off the fantastic building. "This is awesome," he said.

"You're supposed to have your mind on us, not the building."

He hugged her closer and whispered, "I am thinking of you, and our new adventure. I love you, Tianna. When you were the Indian Princess, I wanted you so bad, but you paid no attention to me. Now I have you in my arms and I never want to lose you."

"You won't; I promise." She stretched her neck and kissed him passionately. The tempo of the band changed to a Charleston with the band playing *Runnin' Wild*. Charlie watched her as she threw her beautiful, long black hair back and danced.

"Come on, Charlie. You can do the Charleston, can't you?"

Not to be out done, he kept up with her every move.

At the end of the song he hugged her and asked, "Can we go outside now?"

"Yes." She led the way and together they walked around the huge building, laughing and talking. An alley ran behind the Vanity Ballroom, and Tianna pointed toward two antique Coke bottles with straws, sitting on a beautiful Indian blanket.

"Nice touch," Charlie said as he led her to the blanket. They sat down and sipped their sodas. He laid back, and she snuggled next to him. "Are we getting closer to home base?" she questioned with a laugh.

"I don't know about you, but I sure am."

They kissed passionately. Charlie was excited and could hardly control himself. He opened the top of her blouse as she undid his belt and zipper. Her hand worked its way down, and she smiled.

"I'm going to enjoy this."

Out of the corner of his eye, he saw an emaciated young girl standing next to them. He directed Tianna's attention to the ghostly figure.

"Can she see us?" He asked.

Before Tianna could speak, the girl bent down and touched her arm.

"No!" Tianna screamed and vanished.

Charlie jumped up and cried out. "Tianna."

He ran around the alley, into and through the ballroom, and back to the alley, searching for her, and finally he awoke in the upstairs bedroom where they had remained seated. He turned the lamp on, but Tianna was not there. With panic in his heart, he rushed downstairs into his grandmother's arms.

"Grandma, Tianna is gone. We were in the realm and a ghost took her. Oh God, she's gone. Oh God, what did I do?" He broke into tears and collapsed on the couch, sobbing.

CHAPTER 41

Carol gathered her team, and Charlie explained where he and Tianna were when she vanished. Harry suggested that perhaps the ghost that touched her was seeking help and inadvertently broke the time stream.

"I can understand how that could happen, but why did she vanish from the bedroom? Breaking the stream usually results in our returning to this time, and why was there a ghost in the realm?"

"Perhaps we should trace the timeline back to when she was taken. I could go with you for support." suggested Harry.

"I don't know if you can come with me, Harry. I think it's possible, but it's been so long since I was in the realm on my own. I was there in my previous lives, but this time around Tianna took me there."

Harry studied his young friend. He could see how much Charlie loved Tianna, and he wished he could give him hope for her safe return.

"Charlie, I am sure Tianna can take care of herself, but I think we should go into the Realm and search for her. Can you locate the exact moment when she encountered the ghost?"

"I think so. Let's get ready to try."

Before the two could prepare for the trip back, Jonathon rushed into the room. "Hey, you need to come outside."

It was dusk, and there was a storm brewing. Harry grabbed his jacket and followed Charlie and Carol's team outside. A soft mist of rain made everything gray and forbidding. Jonathon pointed toward the woods behind the empty graveyard. There stood Tianna with seven young women at her side. They were spirits... ghosts with the look of death on their faces and wearing tattered 1930s clothing.

Tianna watched as Carol's team approached. She held her finger up, indicating that they should stop for a moment.

Without speaking, she said to Charlie. They were stuck in the realm, and I couldn't just leave them there.

"God, Tianna. I thought you were dead." Charlie said.

"I know, I didn't expect to be teleported, into the woods." She gathered the seven women around her and softly explained who Charlie was. They looked at him and smiled. A knowing smile.

Carol asked, "Charlie, why is Tianna standing there? What's going on?"

Charlie turned to Harry and asked, "Do you see the ghosts standing next to Tianna?"

"Yes I do, but I don't think anyone else sees them." Harry was surprised that he could see these ghosts. He thought that his ability to see ghosts would be gone, like the memories of the bodies he thought he buried in his backyard.

They approached Tianna and the new ghosts. "Charlie and Harry, these are some friends I picked up. I haven't identified them yet, but I think we have a new adventure ahead of us."

Charlie and Harry looked at each other and began laughing. Harry turned toward Carol and Roger. "Guys, we have to fix this before we can call our work done."

Carol approached them. "Fix what?"

"Tianna brought home seven ghosts, all young women. We have to find out how they died so we can guide them home."

"And who is paying for this new job?"

Harry insisted, "I am, so don't worry about it, dear."

Carol cringed at that name. "It's Carol, Harry. Deer are the wild animals that men hunt."

"Yes. I know." he winked at Charlie. "Roger, you better start taking more notes. I have the feeling your new novel isn't complete yet."

To Be Continued.

If you liked this book,
you will love the author's other novels.

In Search Of Elysium

Kevin Carpenter is learning disabled. In a touching adventure he leads his friends on a search for God, taking them deep into space, in search of a planet called Elysium.

Death on the Point

The Blackwell Series - 1

Colton Blackwell, a football star and teenage detective, stars in this fast moving mystery series; a humorous and romantic novel filled with action and adventure

Blood Bath

The Blackwell Series - 2

Colton Blackwell is faced with another murder. The humor, romance, and adventure continues.

Deadly Sixteen

The Spirit Walker Series - 1

This reincarnation story takes you through the history of Detroit investigating a 300 year murder mystery.

Doyle Mysteries

No. 1 - The Scent Of Murder

Doyle, a retired police detective and master chef, and his Bloodhound (Copper) face a life filled with luxury and murder. A cozy mystery for all ages.

www.duanewurst.com
duanewurst.com@gmail.com

Share your opinion and do a review.

Made in the USA
Columbia, SC
20 May 2022

60599707R00117